The Fattest Mormon

The Winnebago Chronicles Volume 1

Tyson Abaroa

First edition.

ISBN-13: 978-1978173248

For Mandi

Disclaimer

This is the fictional narrative of a fictional character on a fictional weight loss program created by a fictional personal trainer. This is not a weight loss book. It is a novel. Do not attempt to use this book for weight loss advice.

Chapter 1

I couldn't keep chewing. Grease and cheese covered my lips and fingers, with drips rolling down my chin and arms. I could barely hold my head up. I needed to lie down. Sitting up in the metal folding chair kinked my digestive system.

The crowd roared, calling the name of the frat kid with the ten over his head. Then the girl in a tight shirt and short shorts erased the white board she held, changing the number to eleven.

My eyes rolled when I sucked oxygen through my nose, filling my nostrils with the smell of meat and bun. I almost gagged. Then my exhausted throat swallowed the last of the chewed up meat, cheese, and bread. A hand appeared from my left, dropping my ninth Juicy Lucy in front of me. I moaned looking at it. A gurgle ran through my intestines and up through my stomach.

I squinted at the burger in front of me. "I'm bigger than you," I whispered. My hands slowly grabbed it, inching the burger to my mouth. My mouth opened wide, then chomped down into the ground dead cow. The melted cheese cooked inside two patties of burger exploded into my cheeks. Some of it dribbled out the sides of my mouth. I willed myself to take another bite, then another.

After I forced myself to swallow the bites, an air horn blared across the park. Our fifteen minutes had ended. I looked along the field of competitors. We sat at long tables under the giant Paul Bunyan and Babe, his blue ox. The promoter had set up the tables in a V so we could see each other. A skimpy-clothed girl with a dry erase board stood behind each of us. Behind the huge statues, gentle waves from Bemidji Lake brushed against the shore. The frat kid's number had turned to twelve. The closest number to his was my nine. Someone a few seats away had an eight. I looked down at the half-eaten burger, almost gagging.

A group of college boys wearing red shirts with Phi Kappa symbols rushed the tables, hoisting the winner in the air. His head bobbled back and forth. One of the boys grabbed the big two-thousand-dollar check for him, and the group carried him toward the road, placing him in a wheelbarrow.

I didn't watch him roll away. In a daze, I wiped my greasy hands to accept a small envelope from a fat man with a mustache. I opened it to find an eight-hundred-dollar check. I grunted, okay with the amount. The old lady I'd pre-paid to drive me back to the hotel found me in the crowd. She pulled my hand through the park, helping me into her dirty red sedan. I had picked her because I thought she would be a slow driver. The second time she whipped around a corner, churning my stomach, I realized I'd made a mistake.

She slammed on the brakes in front of the hotel. I stumbled out of the car, dragging my feet through the sliding door. A loud rumble from deep in my stomach announced my arrival.

***

The afternoon sun found a crack in the curtains and shone on my face. I sat up, staring at the hotel wall, another ugly hotel wall. I couldn't remember where this wall was or why I'd woken up facing it. I stared at beige wallpaper with green diamonds every four inches down and every foot across. A painting hung on the wall—not really a painting, but a copy of a painting. It wasn't even special, just a vase with some red flowers. I didn't like paying more than sixty dollars a night for a hotel, so I knew I couldn't expect more than a random picture of flowers.

My phone began to buzz and vibrate on the cheap nightstand. The screen lit up with the word MOM. Crap.

"Hi, Mom," I said, mustering some excitement.

"Hi, honey. It's been two weeks since I've heard from you," she chided in her nasally Chicago accent.

"Sorry, just been on the road." I looked at a water stain on the ceiling. She thought I was some big-deal salesman. That was my fault since, well, that's exactly what I kept telling her. Coming from a dad who'd dedicated his life to the grocery store he ran, me being a guy who chased prize money just didn't seem to live up to his legacy of hard work and commitment.

"Have you made any big sales?" she prodded.

"Oh, here and there," I said, tugging at the collar of my stained white undershirt.

"Who knew selling life insurance would keep you away so much?" she said with that mom voice that tries to evoke guilt for not being around so much.

"Well, you know, it's somewhat old school. Sort of door-to-door type stuff."

Then the urge hit me. My stomach contracted then loosened enough to let out a long rumble. I grimaced when all the muscles in my left leg spasmed in urgency.

"Hey, Mom, I'm at an appointment I love you and I'll call you soon," I forced through gritted teeth.

"Okay, I love you too—"

My thumb punched the red button on the screen and I jumped out of bed. I couldn't run to the bathroom, but couldn't walk fast enough. It took a second rumble in my stomach to remember why I had chosen a hotel room with real plumbing. Though I hadn't won the two-thousand-dollar eating prize, my eight-hundred-dollar second place award was enough. I figured with the fuel and hotel I netted six hundred dollars. Adding that to the third place Fargo Hill Body Roll payout of nine hundred two days before, I didn't feel so bad about my north central voyage.

After finishing my business, I walked out of the bathroom and shut the door. A small twinge of guilt hit me as I thought of the poor maid who would have to go in there. But it wasn't my fault the hotel owner was too cheap to install a vent.

At the window I pushed the maroon drapes apart a little to check on my house. My Winnebago Brave rested on the asphalt four stories beneath me. It was cream with a yellow edge around the bottom. A gray *W* decorated the passenger window, underlined by a thin gray line that wrapped around the motorhome.

A gray canopy of clouds sat over the town. Wind brushed the branches of the trees outside. From my view a mile away from Lake Bemidji in Minnesota, I saw the wind gusts creating white caps. Big Canadian Geese struggled against the wind.

Slumping down at the room's table, I ran a hand over my prickly face. I preferred a five-o'clock shadow since it covered up my old acne scars. I rested my chin on my palm, then ran it up into my dirty blond hair. Then I shook my head free of sleep. Hopefully after twelve hours of sleep, my brown eyes had cleared up.

I yawned as I opened my laptop and clicked on the software developed by a guy who'd owed me a favor. It was a simple set of windows without fancy icons or images. He'd made it bare bones as the most efficient way for me to search the most prize money competitions posted on the web. The software asked for the parameters and I typed in two thousand dollars.

After the drive in the laptop hummed, a long list popped up with options to choose from. I clicked on one that displayed a three-thousand-dollar prize, and a flier opened to a boring-looking quilt competition. The next one read five thousand in Nova Scotia. I grimaced. After the last time, I could never go back to Nova Scotia. Memories of running down the main street of Avonlea Village in nothing but a speedo in the dead of winter flashed through my mind before I returned to scanning the list.

A big number caught my eye. "Eight grand?" I questioned out loud. That amount was worth an immediate click. A PDF opened up, displaying the information I wanted.

Taylor-Snowflake Fitness Association
Open to all.
Weight Loss Competition
$8,000 to the person that can lose the most weight percentage.
Start good habits before the holiday pounds creep on. Official Weigh-in September 7th. Final Weigh-in will be after an obstacle mud race on November 15th.
Brought to you by the Taylor-Snowflake Fitness Association.

"Open to all?" I mumbled. "Amateurs."

I raised my pointer finger to about the level of my eyes and looked up at the ceiling. My finger wrote numbers in the air to help calculate in my head. "August twenty-eighth today, two or three days' drive . . . I'm probably two twenty-something right now, maybe squeeze on a few pounds in a couple of weeks." I dropped my hand on the desk. I looked at the postcard of a Japanese Buddhist Temple laying next to my laptop and a smile curled at my lips. I ran to the old tan hotel phone and dialed the front desk.

"Yes, this is Phil Carroll, room 328. Please connect me to Papa John's. Thank you." I looked around the room as I waited to be connected. When I heard the phone click I didn't wait for the person to speak. "I need a large with double meat, double cheese, breadsticks, a cookie pizza, and a root beer."

After I put the ancient receiver back on the cradle I turned back to my laptop. With a click and a mouse swipe, I opened Facebook and searched for friends near Taylor or Snowflake, Arizona. I fist pumped when I found that my old friend, Lee Akiyama, miraculously lived in Taylor. I chuckled, because Lee owed me.

Chapter 2

At full steam, the Winnebago hummed over the last stretch of highway that led to Taylor, Arizona. On either side of the gray weathered asphalt, I saw the dry golden grass of a high plateau desert. Hills and bluffs dotted with giant green bushes stretched across the horizon under a cloudless bright blue dome. A sudden movement to my left caught my eye. About fifteen antelope began bounding away from the highway. Driving on, seemingly untouched grassland gave way to ranches on both sides of the road.

The giant slab of sandstone with the word *Taylor* and the population pushed the pain in my back from sitting for hours to the back of my mind. I slid another Zinger from the box with my free hand and opened it with my teeth. I felt the sugar in the frosting grind on my teeth.

When I'd done more searching on Lee, I was surprised to find him teaching. It stung to remember that Tony "Flip" Gonzalo had banished me from his jiu-jitsu system. *Banishment* is an odd word, but I'd been the first to ever make him contemplate kicking someone out, and it was the only word he could think of in his curse-filled scream session about honesty and integrity. I didn't see what the big deal was. So Lee and I had thrown a match in an important tournament. It was for a good cause.

Finding Lee couldn't have been easier. Typing in MMA or jiu-jitsu in Southern California and expecting specific results would have been silly. But searching in a hick town in Nowhere, Arizona only came up with one result.

The Bago shook turning off of Main Street into the pothole-ridden parking lot in front of some grocery store called a Basha's. Lee's place sat at the corner of the strip mall. The parking spaces were too small and too few for me to leave the house. I maneuvered to the back of the building to park behind a food delivery truck.

A Mexican leaned against the side of the vehicle smoking, listening to Norteño country blaring from the cab. Two other Mexicans walked from the back of the truck into an open door, carrying the truck's supplies. It being my fastest route, I walked to the truck, grabbed a ten-pound bag of rice, and followed them into a steam-filled kitchen that smelled like Pine-Sol. I placed the bag of rice on a short stainless steel table. The two Mexicans I'd followed jumped when they turned to find me. Their faces twisted in confusion.

"*Hola.* I, uh, thought you'd like some help." That did little to untwist their faces. "Well, see you later." I brushed past them to push through a door into a small dining room. I only counted about four tables and four booths. Along one wall, there was a bar about eight feet long with five stools and sneeze glass. The bonsai tree at one end of the bar and the Japanese flag pinned to the wall behind it were all I needed to tell me I'd just walked into a sushi place. I found a short old Asian man busy behind the bar prepping his ingredients. He had a silver comb-over and a dark mustache.

"*Konnichi-wa.*" I smiled.

He smiled back and gave me a "Howdy" in a perfect western accent.

The stool creaked a little when I sat to stare at the bonsai tree. The man smiled at me. He reached over the sneeze guard to hand me a small set of scissors. The thickest part of the trunk leaned to one side of the ceramic pot and had a long branch that reached to the other side of the pot. Three patches of leaves grew out of the branches.

"If you don't mind rounding it out," the old man said, then turned back to his work.

I thought about how strange it was that the old man suddenly trusted a perfect stranger with his plant while I opened and closed the scissors. I thought about my plan of attack, and then I began snipping at the small leaves that poked out. As I finished, I finally noticed the little man standing next to me inspecting my work.

"Well done," he whispered. "You look beautiful."

"What?" I recoiled.

"I was talking to the tree" He frowned. "You gotta talk to the plants. I used to be a farmer. When the crops first sprouted, I'd walk through as much of the field as I could to sing to them."

"What did you sing?" I imagined some ancient Japanese ritual as he walked knee-deep in water through rice paddies.

"Janis Joplin."

"Oh?" My forehead wrinkled.

"The First Lady of Rock and Roll," he said, returning to the serving side of the bar. "California's central valley was *pretty* crazy in the sixties. A bunch of us hippies bought some farms for our communes. That didn't work out so well. When we finally sobered up they all left, but I stayed on planting crops."

"Oh. Okay, well I need to get going. Unless you have something deep-fried?"

"Not ready to cook. We'll open in an hour."

"Maybe I'll be back. The jiu-jitsu place is close by, right?" I felt turned around coming through the back of the building.

"Outside, next door to the right." He began chopping celery.

I walked outside and found a storefront with big bright purple letters reading *Jiu-jitsu*. The glass door swung open to the blaring *beep-beep-beep-beep* of a timer. Rusty steel folding chairs lined the windows with faded black letters on the back. I could only make out the word *Ward* on them. Green wrestling mats covered most of the space except for one corner with a bench, weights and powerlifting rack. An American flag hung on one wall, while Brazilian and Japanese flags hung on the opposite wall. The pungent smell of sweat filled the room.

"Head up!" I heard Lee shout. "Good shot! Break him down!"

I watched two teenage boys grapple on the mat with their arms locked around each other. Each played a game of chess, trying to think three moves ahead of the other. The boys were small and light, grunting and spinning as each kept transitioning from bottom to top and back. Neither attempted a submission. They were both trying to secure a dominant position from which to work. My chest went tight watching them, thinking of the old days, wanting to jump on the mat and mix it up with them. On some of my trips I'd find a random gym to drop in. But it was nothing like being a regular member of a gym.

Beep-beep-beep-beep.

"Good work today, everyone," Lee said.

I watched Stanley Akiyama, or just Lee, smile. It looked like his dark brown eyes were closed, and his sweaty black hair glistened. He was short but had stout arms and legs.

Everyone gave each other a hug, sweat dripping on the mats as they patted each other's backs. After his students filtered passed me out of his storefront, Lee disappeared into a back closet. He returned rolling a mop bucket to the edge of the mat to begin mopping up puddles of sweat. He focused on the mats as he stepped back and forth, wiping the mat with the gray mop.

"You were always a clean freak," I said as I leaned against the wall watching him.

Lee's head shot up to look at me. "Phil? Phil Carroll?"

"Yeah buddy, it's me."

"I haven't seen you in about . . ."

"Years," I finished for him. "How did you end up in a town like this?"

"You remember that girl, the one you threw that grappling match so I could impress her?" he reminded me.

"Yeah."

"We're married. She grew up here and wanted to come back. The town lacked a sushi place and a gym. So . . ."

"Great! I'm glad I could help you with your marriage! That's your sushi place next door too?" I asked. "The Sushi Stop? I thought I met the owner."

"Yep, they call this the Japanese corner," he said smiling. "My uncle Tim primarily runs the restaurant. He got too old to be farming in Visalia, so I had someone teach him to roll sushi. I figured an old Japanese guy behind the bar was a better image than one of my Mexican cooks."

"Isn't that racist?" I wondered.

"Well, maybe. But it's marketable. When parents drop their kids off for jiu-jitsu they go next door and grab a roll or two."

"Clever. How's the game in the town?" I asked, referring to his talent pool.

"The boys from around here are great. Corn-bred and -fed kids just like those Iowa wrestling kids who used to come into the Riverside gym and throw their weight around. So what are you doing here?" he asked as he finished mopping.

I pulled out a crumpled copy of the flier for the weight loss competition. The muscles around my eye twitched because I didn't know how he might respond.

"Buddy." Lee looked up at me with a frown when he figured out what I was proposing. "I'm honest now. I may not be one, but I married a Mormon. I know they didn't specify that you had to be from here, but these are good people. Look." He flipped the flier over, pointing to his jiu-jitsu logo. "I'm one of the sponsors. I'm hoping to use it to get some more people over here."

"Good, and won't it help if everyone sees that the winner comes out of your gym?" I suggested.

"Winner? You know I can't train you. If Flip found out you were even here right now, he'd pull his affiliation so fast. After that stunt we pulled, it took me two years just to get back on his good side and get permission to run my own gym. I basically had to escape here and send him videos of me teaching every week. Then I had to spend a month with him and all the guys in SoCal. A juvey court put me on probation as a teenager for trying to steal a car. *That* was better than what he put me through."

"Well, I'm sorry that terrible stunt hitched you up with your wife. And yes, Flip banished me, but the way I see it is that you run your own restaurant and gym, and have a happy life because of me. I'm the one who lost it all."

I watched Lee's shoulders drop. He looked down at the floor. "Fine, but no classes with everyone else. You'll go under the guise of private lessons. I don't want you corrupting these kids."

"You know private sessions won't do as much." I scoffed. Just rolling with one guy in private was a good workout, but being able to train with multiple people would make me work harder and burn more calories.

"Okay, but just the two weekly advanced classes. Flip would kill me if he found out." He ran his hands through his black hair. "Why didn't you just apologize?"

"For what? Everyone in that tournament saw all the revolutionary techniques *he* came up with in action. You and I basically put on a clinic for all the other students in the area," I argued.

"Yeah, but he didn't like that it was dishonest. And he's right. Our match was a lie. He knew you and I weren't really trying. I got the lecture from him about it. I spent weeks trying to get him to lift the ban. And he spent weeks drilling honest competition into me." Lee suddenly shuddered.

"Okay, I'm sorry you had to go through all that," I said sincerely, thinking about how it must have hurt Lee. He was always more serious about the game than me. I used to compete just to win the samurai sword they would hand out as a trophy, because samurai swords are cool.

"Thank you, and I'm sorry you look so fat," he said, poking me in the belly.

"Perfect. Weigh-ins are next week and I need you to cook for me. You still make sweet and sour chicken?"

"I'm Japanese and run a sushi place; you just asked for Chinese food." He rolled his eyes.

"Chicken Katsu will work," I said, shrugging.

"Fine, come over tonight. Where are you staying?"

"For now?" I asked with a gritted, forced smile. One eyebrow went up. "Out back?"

"Out back? What do you mean?" I followed him as he walked over the mats and to the rear exit. When he pushed open the door, he froze when he saw what I meant. In the back driveway of the shopping center sat my Winnebago, dusty from crossing the country. Splattered bugs caked the windshield. He really would have called me fat had he seen the inside, filled with Little Debbie boxes and wrappers.

"Home sweet home."

"I guess this means you also need a driveway?"

A honk blared through the driveway. We turned to see a Basha's delivery truck trying to get my RV to move. I pushed past Lee and ran out to move it.

"Where am I going?" I shouted back at Lee.

"153 Plum Road!" he yelled.

Before rounding the corner to the door of the Bago I froze. Spinning around I shouted, "Wait!" Lee turned to look at me. "What's a Mormon?"

"Later!"

The truck driver blared his horn again. I waved as I jumped into the vehicle and ran to the driver's seat. I drove back out to Main Street asking my girl Fake Siri for directions. Never staying in one place very long, I just used pre-paid phones. She directed me south down Main Street.

Calling it a small town was an understatement. Taylor, Arizona fit the description of the classic American hick town. Green fields with rocky bluffs surrounded the town. Mom and pop businesses lined the road, except for the Giant gas station. Not giant as in large, Giant the name of the fuel company. Wal-Mart, Sonic, and the Family Dollar were the other chain stores I recognized. Looking past the main streets, I saw that most of the houses were pre-fab or mobile. At the moment, it was just like any other small village I could exploit.

My phone's robot voice told me to turn left down Pinedale Road in one mile. I followed her directions. She pointed me down an empty road that led into golden hills, then had me turn down a gravel road that ended at a single home surrounded by nothing but high desert grassland that looked like a prairie. As I looked out, the open golden grass rippled like waves, making it feel similar to the open prairies I'd crossed countless times on the Great Plains leading up to the Rocky Mountains. I pulled into the driveway of a tidy one-story gray house with white trim and a white picket fence.

A woman came out of the house, walking right up to my RV. Her grave face stared at me. I couldn't really read her outside of the small grimace she had. I turned off the RV, feeling nervous as I hopped out of the door on the side. I could feel my stomach tighten. My face flexed like I might get punched. When I walked around the RV, I saw Lee's wife, Elizabeth, standing with her arms crossed and tapping her foot on the cracked cement. My heart sank, anticipating a scolding.

"Phil Carroll, I don't know if I should hit you or hug you," she stated. Elizabeth had black hair cut at her shoulders. Her light blue eyes were glaring at me. She had big round lips painted a bright red in a deep contrast to her fair skin and dark hair. She wore a black long-sleeved t-shirt, dark blue skinny jeans, and light blue Toms.

"Usually, women . . . do both," I said, trying to lighten the mood. It didn't work; she kept staring at me with pursed lips. The sides of her mouth were twitching.

"Lee just called and told me you were on your way. You know you made Lee's life hell for a while?" Her foot continued tapping the ground.

"Uh, because of his trouble with Flip," I joked, "or because he married you?" I gave her a goofy smile, hoping it would go over the right way.

I cringed a little when her eyes squinted. I thought I had really stepped in it. But my heart began to beat again at her reaction. First, the edges of her mouth slowly curled. Then her big red lips parted, showing her teeth. "Both," she laughed and opened her arms for a hug. She walked over to me and threw her arms around me. She pinned my arms to my sides, patting me on the back.

"It's been a long time, Lizzie." I struggled to hug her back.

She pushed away sternly and punched my arm. "Yes, he was in trouble. But that little con job you talked him into did eventually bless him with me. And her." She pointed to a little barefoot girl in pigtails, a pink shirt, and jeans. The girl ran up and wrapped her arms around Lizzie's leg. I could tell she looked much more like Lee than like Lizzie, with Japanese black hair and brown eyes.

"You're welcome," I responded, trying to remind her she owed it to me. "And this is?" I leaned over, extending my hand.

"Aiko," the little girl squeaked, burying her face in Lizzie's leg.

"Are you hungry?" Lizzie asked. "Lee mentioned something about feeding you."

"No. But I *do* need to eat," I said with a grin.

"Uh oh, that sounds like quite the story. Come inside."

I followed Lizzie off the driveway and over a walkway made with flat red and pink stones. I took a step onto the porch and found two rocking chairs overlooking the wide grasslands. I turned around to see the view. Giant white clouds were gliding over the open golden hills.

"It's beautiful at sunset," Lizzie said. "That's why Lee bought this plot." She turned, entering the house.

Walking in and finding yellow walls and family pictures felt different. I had grown accustomed to my tiny RV, cheap motel wallpaper, and fake paintings of flowers. Kids' toys were all over the floor. *My Little Pony* blared from the TV. Lizzie led me through the open living room and into the kitchen.

She pointed to a stool at the granite island of the kitchen. I obeyed the gesture and sat down. She opened the fridge to see what she had available. "Okay, I have some leftover meatloaf, some cold cuts for a sandwich, or some frozen burritos. Pick your poison."

With a smile, I pulled the competition flier out and pushed it across the granite to her. I watched Lizzie pick it up and laugh out loud. "One of everything, please," I said when she looked at me.

Her eyes were wide. "Am I participating in a Phil Carroll long con?"

"I prefer the term 'professional miscellaneous competitor'?" I forced a smile and tipped my head, hoping she'd buy that.

"Sounds to me like you're more of a 'liar'?" she questioned, tilting her head and forcing a smile back to mock me.

"Would you settle for a professional hustler?" I asked.

"Oh dear," she said. "This means you're going to eat me out of house and home. Do I get any of that eight thousand?"

"I'll eat everything I can until September seventh, and then I'll be on strict half-rations," I said. I bit my lip, dreading the day I'd actually have to start losing weight. The fun part would be all the eating. "But I'll financially compensate you for any crumb I take from you."

Lizzie smiled. "That sounds interesting. One ham, meatloaf, burrito sandwich coming right up."

"With mayo, please," I chuckled.

***

I finally called my mom that night.

"Honey, when are you coming home?" she demanded.

"I'm not sure. See, the company just sent me down to Arizona. I'll be down here a few months."

"Months?" she screeched.

"Yeah, I'm in this town called Taylor. Would you imagine? Only one person in five here has life insurance. So I have a nice little market here to really sell some good stuff."

"That's odd, but you need to check in with me more. Your father, God rest him, would have your hide for abandoning me so much."

"Mom," I said.

"Don't you "mom" me. I spent all that time vomiting while I was pregnant with you. Then I wiped your bum for years . . ." She went on, listing everything a mom is supposed to do.

"Mom," I repeated.

"What?"

"I have a big day tomorrow, a lot of walking door to door."

"Okay, well, be good and I love you."

"Love you too. Good night."

Chapter 3

I was lying in bed watching an old samurai movie when I felt the vibrations of someone pounding on the door. I thought it was the wind at first. A small tub of rainbow swirl sherbet ice cream rested on my chest. It excited me to tilt my head and see my belly sticking out between my boxers and undershirt. My paunch blocked the keys of my computer as it sat on my lap.

Fortunately, my strategy was making me fatter. Some research had gotten me set up on an ideal schedule to pack on some pounds. I had been in town for only three days and had gained five pounds. It started when I'd looked up sumo wrestlers. Like me, most people probably don't know how strenuous their schedule is. They spend all morning doing drills, exercises, and wrestling. Their first meal, which is huge, is lunch, and then they nap all afternoon. So I'd tried to start something similar. I would go for a short jog and then train at Lee's morning jiu-jitsu class. I helped move food from delivery trucks into his sushi joint after class. The activity was just enough to famish me. After class I'd eat a huge bowl of his noodles and fried chicken. Lee would drive me home and I'd sleep all afternoon and then have dinner with Lee, Lizzie, and Aiko. There may have been a few dozen fig bars after that too.

Vibrations from the pounding on the door snapped me out of my TV trance. I got up and ran to the door thinking something might be on fire. I shivered a little when my bare feet hit the linoleum floor of my Winnebago. Lee waited for me in slacks, a green button-down shirt, and a tie, smiling up at me.

"Lee, it's eight thirty. What are you doing?"

"You're coming to church with us, buddy."

"Uh, no," I said, releasing the door in his face.

Lee caught the door before it closed and followed me in. "It smells like three-day-old pizza." He looked around and lifted a shirt off the couch. "Ah, that's a box of three-day-old pizza."

"It's *day*-old pizza and it's probably still good," I protested. "You can have some," I added, leaning against the laminate counter of my kitchen set.

"It's fast Sunday . . . so yes," he said, taking a piece.

"What's that mean, a shorter service?" I asked hopefully.

"Lizzie doesn't let me eat around her until afternoon. Mormons don't eat one day a month," Lee said with a mouthful of stiff pizza. He sat at the swivel chair of the small table next to the door. Lee kicked his shined dress shoes onto the table. I walked over and smacked them off.

"Manners!" I said. "Not eating for a whole day? That's kind of crazy," I thought out loud.

"Anyway," Lee said. He stood up with another piece of pizza then went to each of my windows and opened them up. "You are in fact going to church with us. Lizzie's orders. And if I have to go to church to make her happy, then you have to go to church, buddy." He chomped at the pizza again and looked around. "Hey, the boxy outside makes it look like it's straight out of the seventies, but this is all pretty new."

"Yeah, Winnebago made a throwback model. It looks like what they produced decades ago, but it's stocked with all the modern toys," I told him.

"So how much was it?" he asked.

I sat on the couch and put my hands behind my head. "To launch it, the knuckleheads held a competition. Whoever could stay in contact with it the longest kept it. So I lay down with my leg against the tire and waited. Three days later, they handed me the keys," I said with a smile.

"Wow," Lee said, taking another bite of pizza.

"So, I don't have nice clothes. I guess I can't go." I tried making an excuse.

"Do you have jeans?" Lee asked me with a smile.

"Yeeees," I forced out.

"Do you have any button-down shirts?"

"Maybe. Does a cowboy shirt count?" I started thinking of the dark blue Wrangler shirt I'd ended up with in Amarillo. After eating the seventy-two-ounce steak at the Big Texan in Amarillo, I was so full I still didn't remember how that shirt had gotten wrapped around my head.

"Then you'll fit right in!"

"But—"

He cut me off. "Lizzie has been feeding you, washing your clothes, and letting you watch TV in the afternoon with Aiko. I have been letting you come to morning classes. And you're using my electricity and my septic tank. So you're coming to church. Three hours for me, three hours for you too."

I lifted my fingers in the air and started calculating. "Buying food for a few months, about sixty dollars a week. Free classes, probably seventy; TV twenty; electricity . . ."

"Oh man," Lee interrupted. "You still do that sky calculator thing?

While he spoke he was going through my tiny cupboards and closet. He found and sprayed a can of air freshener. The mist filled my lungs, causing me to gag and cough.

"Wait, three hours?" I asked when the bitter taste of Lysol cleared my mouth.

"Yep, that's how Mormons do it. Now, get dressed," he said.

"I don't want to."

"Oh, you really do."

"Why?"

"The ward's having a break-the-fast." Lee smiled big.

"I'm still not quite sure what you mean by *fast*. What's a break-the-fast?"

He rolled his eyes. "So the first Sunday of every month, Mormons don't eat for a whole day." He looked at me to see if I understood, then continued when I nodded. "Sometimes they end the church service with a big potluck called a break-the-fast."

"Wait," I demanded. "You technically fast at night. Is that where we get the word *breakfast*?"

"Yes," Lee said as he sat back at the table behind the co-pilot's seat. "Just think of it, buddy, two twelve-foot tables put together with Crock-Pots full of food. And there are rolls, cakes, cookies." Lee extended his arms. "Just, so much food, everywhere."

I thought about all the potential calories. I ran a finger down the gray tubing of my tan pleather couch. "I'm in!" I told him. I jumped up to take off my clothes.

"Wait till I'm gone!" Lee shouted at me.

It only took a few minutes for me to shower, needing only some soap and a spot of shampoo. When I finished, it surprised me to find Lee now on my couch. He'd kicked back with a bowl of cereal and my laptop, watching my movie. With a towel around my waist, I walked to my room.

"I thought you were leaving," I called as I began buttoning the metal snaps of my cowboy shirt.

"I was still hungry. You still watch this crap?"

"Of course. I want to grow up to be a samurai." I glanced over at the postcard from Japan taped to my closet door.

"I almost got Lizzie's family hooked on this stuff. Lizzie wouldn't let me watch swords cutting people's heads off once Aiko came," he said with milk dribbling out of his mouth. "But how do I teach her to cheer for whoever represents the Asian persuasion? How do I teach her to appreciate my heritage without samurai swords and ninja movies?"

"I'm sorry, weren't you born and raised in Bakersfield? And you didn't even start martial arts until you started college."

"After I took an Asian heritage class." Some more milk droplets dribbled from his mouth.

"Dude, not on the computer!" I yelled, sitting on my bed to put on socks. After my socks were on I realized something. I looked at the decaying running shoes next to my bed. "Um," I yelled through the door. "I don't have nice shoes."

"I know what you need," Lee shouted. I heard him drop the bowl into the sink. The door opened then slammed shut. I slid into my slippers and followed him to the house just as Lizzie and Aiko walked out.

"You look ready for a rodeo," Lizzie said. She'd tied her black hair in a ponytail, and she wore a dark crimson dress matching her dark shade of lipstick. Aiko ran out onto the lawn in pigtails. She had on a green dress with puffy sleeves.

Lee ran out the front door smiling a little too much about something behind his back. I watched him like he was about to attack me. He shouted in triumph when he dropped a pair of black cowboy boots by one of the rocking chairs.

I sat down and began tugging them on. "They're a little tight."

Lee laughed. "That's how they're supposed to be. Don't forget this." He walked behind the rocking chair, flipped my collar up, and snapped my top button. I heard something rub on leather, and then it tightened around my neck. When I stood up I looked down and saw a big turquoise rock over my top button with two leather strands running down my chest.

"Bolo ties are pretty fashionable in these parts, pilgrim," Lee said, attempting to imitate John Wayne.

Lizzie laughed as I tried to look at my reflection in the window.

"Let's get this over with," I growled.

Chapter 4

Lee had lied to me. Not a single person wore cowboy clothes in the Mormon meeting. All the women and girls wore nice dresses. The men and boys donned suits or white shirts and ties.

"I thought the Startup family would be here," he tried to explain.

I fidgeted all through their first hour. Some bald guy in a suit with thick black glasses conducted, as they said, but he never really said anything. They sang as a group a bunch of times. I began thinking that maybe Lee had lied to me about the break-the-fast when I only ended up with a small piece of bread.

After the first meeting finally ended, the Mormons attacked me. Two kids about twenty years old came out of nowhere and began talking to me. Then some large man with a belly hanging over his belt extended big meaty hands, squeezing mine white. He said something about being a mission leader. Then the bald man who had led the meeting found me and told me he was the bishop. More people surrounded me, introducing themselves.

"So what do you think of church?" Lizzie asked me, leading me out of the big room and into a hall.

"Was it a funeral?"

"No, it was a testimony meeting. Why?"

"Well, I couldn't concentrate with all the kids crying and talking. But when I did look up all I saw were people crying."

"Oh." Lizzie frowned.

By this time my stomach groaned, begging me to find some food. But Lee and Lizzie led me to a room filled with children, where they dropped off Aiko. As the door closed, I caught sight of the old lady that Aiko sat next to. In a canvas bag next to her I saw one of those bags of white and pink frosted animal crackers. I knew where to escape if this whole break-the-fast thing was a trick.

For two more hours I sat around listening to people talk about God. First I went with Lizzie and Lee to an adult class. Some ancient woman asked me to stand and introduce myself. Then she started talking about something in the Bible for almost a whole hour. I almost fell asleep until something that sounded like a siren went off. I jumped to my feet, but Lee, laughing, pulled me back down and explained it was a five-minute buzzer.

Then the men and women split up. I walked with Lee to a room where all the men and teenage boys gathered. Lee joked with one of the boys I recognized as his student. The bald bishop guy had everyone sing, followed by another prayer. Then different men went through some announcements. Again we separated. Groups of old men, boys, and men our age scattered. I was so turned around in that building. If the fire alarm really did go off, I'd have gotten lost and died. Then someone got up and gave a boring lesson on things some dead guy had said about a hundred years ago.

My stomach moaned. I couldn't pay attention to another guy in a white shirt and tie talking about church stuff anymore. I first traced the black lines of the buffed and polished hardwood basketball court our chairs sat on. If I angled my head just right, I could make a spot of the reflection follow the lines. They separated the court by big brown accordion-like dividers.

Then I started counting all the white bricks that made up the walls of what they called the "cultural hall." Cultural? It was just a basketball court. I spent a few minutes observing the folding hoop parallel to the ceiling. It seemed to go up and down with a box of gears and a reel of cables. How was this cultural? At the moment it couldn't even be a basketball court because some guy was talking about the Bible.

Then I smelled it. Something drifted through the air, calling me.

Lee saw me craning my neck, searching for the scent, and hissed at me, "Just fifteen more minutes!"

That quarter of an hour passed so slowly. I just wanted to eat. That whole day I'd had nothing but a few scoops of ice cream. The weigh-in was coming up, and I needed to store away as many calories as I could.

Finally, yet another person said another prayer. I jumped after a loud snap at the back of the room echoed through the hall. Hopefully this is what getting into heaven is like. Two marvelous boys pushed open the brown accordion room divider. That's when I saw it.

Twenty-four feet of food. My mouth watered, staring at a long spread of hissing Crock-Pots. Nothing but different kinds of rolls filled one whole section. I saw bowls of coleslaw, potato salad, and macaroni salad. Lee had lied about one thing. No dessert waited for me on the serving table. The desserts had their own table! About five feet away I saw cookies, brownies, sheet cake, fruit salad, and Jell-O.

"No way!" I drooled.

Unfortunately, Lee made me help set up round tables. Then we brought our chairs to the tables with the other men. Women threw stark white sheets of plastic over the tables. Then, of course, we had to say another prayer.

I had been uncomfortable being the out-of-place guy the whole day. It did have one perk, though. All those people, who had been fasting for a whole day, let me serve myself first. I didn't know, nor did I care, how they felt as I heaped food onto my plate. While everyone else waited in line, I started stuffing my face. I laughed when I saw Lee watching me. He shook his head at seeing the special treatment I got. I thought for a moment that maybe these Mormons were on to something. I could do this every week.

"Hello."

My mouth almost fell open. A vision of a woman sat down across the table from me. She had dark brown hair that fell over one shoulder. Her light blue eyes sparkled under the florescent white lights. She was beautiful. She smiled, the kind of smile that you would vow to do anything to make sure she would always be happy. The kind that would make you walk three miles in the snow to find and kill the last flower, just to bring the dead plant's carcass back to her.

"Hi-oh," I replied with a full mouth. I'd started to say "hi," but then tried to go with "hello" and ended up sounding like an ape. Her smile started to fade. Maybe visions don't look at you with disgust. Then I realized that she could probably see the half-chewed food in my open mouth. There was a brief temptation to spit everything out and start over. I stopped myself just before my tongue pushed it out onto my plate, realizing it would be a terrible idea.

"Keira!" Lizzie called, bringing her food, giving me time to chew. She seemed excited to see her. "Phil, this is my kid sister, Keira! Keira, this is Lee's friend and our cupid, Phil Carroll. Keira is a member of our ward. She lives just up the street."

"Mahaw." I still had too much food in my mouth.

"Oh, *that* Phil?" She even talked pretty. And she knew my name? I didn't quite know what to say. I just watched her.

"Phil? Phil!" I stopped staring when Lizzie snapped her finger in front of my face. "Keira just graduated in kinesiology."

I just sighed and nodded.

Lizzie rolled her eyes. "That means she's a personal trainer." I still didn't understand what she was trying to say. I was too busy looking at the pretty girl. "Keira," Lizzie said, moving on without me, "Phil is living at our house. He just moved in to start, uh, serving at the Sushi Stop."

"I did?"

Lizzie kicked me under the table. "You did, and you're looking to enter that weight loss thing?"

"I did," I said, realizing I need to play along. Even though I wasn't happy that apparently all she could think of as a cover story was to become a waiter. For this dream of a woman, the least she could have done was make me a firefighter, a veterinarian, or an astronaut who had happened to find the cure for cancer while experimenting in the international space station.

Lee sat down with only a scoop of macaroni salad and a few meatballs on his plate. He mumbled through gritted teeth, "You took all the food, you–"

"Language," Lizzie snapped.

"How much do you weigh right now?" the pretty girl asked.

"Hopefully . . ." I caught myself. "Uh, hopefully not more than two-forty."

"Would you like me to help you?" she asked.

"Uh-huh," I said with a sigh, thinking I wanted to run with her anywhere.

"Great, do you want to start tomorrow?" she asked.

"I do," I said, staring at her lips. Lee kicked me and I realized what I had just said. "I mean, darn, I'm going to be helping Lee with some stuff." I turned to him. "You know, that thing we have to do at the place?"

He just crinkled his nose at my vague suggestion.

"Well, let me know." She cut up some of her food. "I'll even make you a deal. You let me train you for a discount if I get to post some before and after shots?"

The word "discount" fired in my brain. By instinct my finger went up in the air. Personal training could be anywhere from thirty to fifty dollars an hour. Even if the discount brought it down to thirty dollars an hour, that could still be over one hundred a week. That could seriously cut into my budget for this trip, despite my odd online jobs. I looked across the table at her smiling at me. All things considered, I wanted to be around her, but that was the only reason to consider training with her.

"I, uh, don't know," I said with a frown.

"Yeah," Lee chimed in. "You know, I've been coaching athletes for years now. I don't see why *I* couldn't train him. Jiu-jitsu burns a ton of calories. I have the space and I know exercises . . ." Seeing the glare she gave, he shut up.

Keira's eyes squinted and her nose flared. "Give me a shot." She pointed at me. "I'll have you pay for three sessions, and then I'll coach you for free through the rest of the competition."

My finger started going back up into the air, but Lee slapped it down. He looked at me with raised eyebrows. Lizzie pursed her lips and gave a slight nod.

"Deal," I said, standing up and offering her my hand. She shook it with a soft manicured hand. I might have held on a little longer than I should have. When she looked down at our hands I quickly let go.

Lee leaned over to me and spoke out of the side of his mouth. "This better be worth it. I just helped you hustle my own sister-in-law!" he whispered against the hum of conversations.

I looked across the table. My chest fluttered when Keira gave me a wink and a smile.

Chapter 5

The next morning, I woke up once again to pounding at my door, swearing when I saw the hands of the clock pointing to five thirty. A weak glow from the morning invaded through the slits of my blinds.

Only my boxers and undershirt were on when I opened the door. Keira looked up at me with her big blue eyes. She'd tied her silky hair back and was wearing a ratty dry wicking t-shirt that read "NAU" and "BattleFrog" under that. She jogged in place with loose running pants.

Even as pretty as she was, I just said, "Why?"

"Day one, brother. Let's go for a jog."

"I . . ." I looked down at dawn reflecting in her face, illuminating small freckles and two subtle dimples at the edge of her smile. "Fine." I let the door slam and went looking for clothes.

I met her wearing some short gym shorts, old running shoes, and a tank top. She smiled at me when I walked out, waking me up some more.

"Can I take your picture?"

"Sure?" I had to remember why. She wanted a "before" picture.

Keira had parked a turquoise and cream Mini Cooper next to my RV. She reached into her pocket to pull out her phone and told me to stand against the wall of my RV. The flash lit up the morning, leaving a bright dot in my vision.

"Okay," she said with a smile as she put her camera away. Then she pulled out a calculator. "How old are you?"

"Thirty-three," I said with a yawn.

"How tall are you?"

"It depends," I smiled.

Her forehead crinkled, "on what?"

"I'm five-ten. When girls are around I can bring my chin down to push the back of my head up a half an inch."

"So five-ten it is." She rolled her eyes.

She then pulled a small scale out of her car. It lit up with red digital zeros when she placed it on the asphalt of Lee's driveway.

"Step on, please."

I stepped on the scale to watch it flash three times with the number 236. I had to stop myself from cursing. I wanted to get to at least 240 before the weigh-in the next night. I could hit my goal with enough food that day and the following. I would also take some Imodium and a half-gallon of water before stepping on the official scale. With careful calculations, I planned how to get as heavy as possible.

"Let's stretch now," she said with a little too much pep as she put the scale away.

"Okay. Could we maybe do some sort of warm-up first, before stretching?"

Her brows furrowed a little. "I know what I'm doing. These are good stretches."

"Sure," I said. Doing jiu-jitsu for years, I'd learned that I hated stretching cold muscles. I guessed a degree meant more than a few centuries of a successful martial art.

"Let's start with what's called cherry pickers," she said, then spread her legs and bent over to teach me how to stretch. I became a little annoyed. I turned when I heard a tapping noise from the house. I grumbled seeing Lee pointing and laughing at me.

"Come on," Keira called, politely ordering me to take part.

I spread my legs and leaned over to begin stretching. She led me through a stretching/yoga routine with a patronizing smile. Every time she would look away I'd roll my eyes. All I could think about was why I had agreed to this. Sure, she was pretty, but I knew what I was doing. I thought about my first weight loss competition. Small stakes, three-week game in Tampa. I grimaced, thinking about jogging in muggy Florida along the beach. Three pounds of baby powder still hadn't protected me very well.

"Okay, let's go running." She snapped me out of my humid memory. "We'll start out slow, then ramp up, and then slow down. I think just a mile today should do it. What do you think?" she asked like a cheerleader.

"Sure." I shrugged my shoulders.

"Come on, get excited!" she cheered as we began running.

I rolled my eyes, then followed her down Lee's cinder road. When we reached the pavement, she had us run a little faster away from town where the road slanted up a small hill. Halfway up the incline she shouted at me to sprint. At the top we turned around, letting gravity bring us back down. We slowed a little when the road evened out.

"That was good. Let's go back up that hill one more time," she said.

"Okay," I said through a deep breath.

I followed her as she turned and said, "Let's race." She sprinted straight up the hill. I didn't allow myself to be more than a few steps behind her.

We were both breathing heavily at the top of the hill. "Time to rest," she suggested, putting her arms behind her head. I just stood watching her with my hands on my hips. It took about a minute to be able to breathe normally again. I was still getting used to the thin air of the Arizona mountains, but other than that, I didn't think I'd done so bad.

And apparently, neither did she. "Great job," she said with a smile. "Now tell me something." I looked at her. The smile turned to a frown. "Why are you lying to me?"

"Uh, I don't know what you mean." I shrugged.

"Someone who really needs a personal trainer would have passed out the first time we ran up this hill."

"Well, I don't know what to say." I started to panic but took a deep breath. "You know, I never really asked you for personal training. You just kind of assumed I . . ."

"Cut it," she demanded. "And tell me the truth. You don't have any idea how much I need this!"

"You need this?" I asked.

"If you'll be honest with me, I'll be honest with you. Does that sound fair?" Keira stuck out her hand.

I looked at her, not knowing what was going on. Her eyes bored into mine.

"Fair?" she repeated.

I hesitated. My mouth opened then closed. I had to think of where her question might take me. "I guess so," I said, shaking her hand.

"Then we have an honesty pact. You go first," she demanded.

I began walking down the hill and she walked next to me. "I don't really need your help," I began. Her jaws clenched. "I'm really just here for the *dinero*. I travel around chasing prize money," I finished.

"That's it?"

"It's a simple life, meager at times, but I've mostly enjoyed it."

We walked on in silence. At the moment she had the upper hand. I was subject to whatever she thought best to divulge. When we reached the bottom of the hill, she finally spoke. "Participants aren't supposed to know, but if the winner has a trainer, the trainer gets two thousand dollars," she said, forcing a smile.

"So, you were hustling me?" I asked in disbelief. *She* had played *me*. I looked at her eyes. They'd seemed so innocent when she'd been pitching her services the day prior.

"And what were you doing?" she asked me.

"Well, I didn't see *that* coming." I scratched at my stubble.

"The fitness association wants to foster some competition. There's a gym in Snowflake. It's run by this jerk that tries to crowd out all his competitors up here. He has all the credibility. I just have my master's degree and a business card right now. I need the money and the reputation to really start my own business. I have student loans collecting interest and no business income to pay them." She bit her thumb knuckle.

"*You* were hustling *me*?" I couldn't get past that. She had completely taken me by surprise. "I guess I've learned a new lesson. Never trust an overanxious personal trainer."

Keira punched me in the arm.

We reached Lee's cinder road. As our feet crunched through the purple volcanic rock, I thought about my options. I wanted the eight grand. She needed the money and the win. As much as I hated partnering up, this one had pretty clear boundaries. Our prizes, if we won, would be separate payouts. Too many people like me lost in a partnership for the same purse. The quick flashing memory of a pretty girl in Reno hit my mind.

"Look, against my better judgment, I'm in. Right now, it's win-win for both of us." We walked up to my RV. "Let's do this. Tomorrow is Tuesday, the night of the weigh-in. I'll meet you there, claim you as my trainer or whatever I have to do. Then on Wednesday morning you start putting me through the ringer. I want money, you need a win. I think we've got this in the bag."

"Okay, thank you," she said.

"Now, I'm going to eat an ice cream sandwich and go back to bed," I said. She looked at me with disgust. "What? You want one? I have a whole box."

She just turned and walked straight to the house. I laughed when I thought about what she would to say to Lizzie and Lee.

***

I was sweaty, grimy, and close to losing all my patience that afternoon when I drove back into Lee's driveway. The RV shuddered when I pulled in. My head hurt, and rubbing my temples didn't help. After swallowing a few pills, I jumped out of the RV to take a big gulp of the fresh mountain air, filling my lungs with dust and the smell of wild grass.

Lee rocked with his eyes closed in one of the chairs on the patio. I walked over to sit in the other chair. Aiko played in the front yard, holding a baby doll and picking at the grass. The big sky was on fire. The setting sun turned the drifting clouds yellow and red. I took another deep breath, soaking in the quiet countryside.

"We got in trouble with Keira this morning," Lee said with his eyes still closed.

"What did she say?"

"She was upset that we helped you hustle her."

"We never actually hustled anyone," I replied. "Yet."

"Yup. Still, wasn't happy about it."

"Did she mention that she hustled us too?" I kicked my feet in front of me and laced my fingers behind my head as I leaned back against the chair.

Lee opened his eyes. "She what?"

I laughed. "Two grand to the trainer with the winning contestant."

Lee looked at me. He watched my face for any reaction. I just closed my eyes, taking another deep breath, feeling the stress melt away.

"Lizzie!" Lee yelled. "Lizzie, Phil has something to tell you!"

We heard footsteps coming to the door. The screen door squeaked as it opened. Lizzie wore an apron and had a messy bun.

"What? Is he finally leaving?" Lizzie raised an eyebrow.

"What did your sister tell you this morning?" I asked, wondering what Keira had made up.

Lizzie rolled her eyes and huffed. "That she was disappointed and that she needed someone she could trust."

"Did she mention what she gets from the organizers if I win?"

"She said she would earn a reputation. If you won, people would come to her, like free advertising."

"She gets money! Go on. Tell her, Phil!" Lee thundered.

"Money?" Lizzie almost choked.

"Apparently," I started, "if the winner has a trainer, the trainer gets two grand."

"That butthead." Lizzie caught herself from saying something else as Aiko ran up.

Something began beeping from the kitchen.

"Dinner's in ten minutes, boys. Then you two get to do the dishes." She spun on her heel, retreating to the kitchen.

"All right, honey," Lee said.

"Thank you," I said as the door slammed.

Lee turned to me. "Huh, so she reverse-hustled us? I just can't get away from people like you," Lee said. He closed his eyes again. "Where'd you go today?"

"The Motor. Vehicle. Division. In Show Low." I shivered thinking of the people I'd had to wait with. I shivered again thinking of the mean people behind the desk.

"Why?" he asked.

I pulled an Arizona driver's license from my pocket and handed it over to him. "Just in case."

"That's my address," he blurted, scratching his head. "I wonder if this means I can claim you as a dependent for my taxes."

We watched the clouds drift. A cool breeze swept over the grassland. The dry grass waved along the hills.

"Do you get tired of it?" Lee asked me as we watched the landscape.

"Tired of what?"

"Drifting."

I thought a moment. "Nope," I lied. It had its benefits, but wandering was growing exhausting.

"You don't think about finding something permanent, a wife, a couple kids, a real job?"

"I mean, I think about it. I just don't think that's my kind of life," I told him.

"I used to think the way we would bounce from grappling tournament to tournament was fun."

I looked at him and asked, "Now?"

"Can't beat the view," he said looking at Aiko.

"You're welcome," I re-informed him.

"Yeah," he snorted. "You're never going to let me forget, are you?"

"Nope."

We kept watching the clouds drift.

"Keira's a good girl," Lee growled.

"I believe it," I said.

"Don't go trying to hook up with her. She's a sister to me, and she's had it rough in the love department."

"I'll be honest, that's why I originally agreed to work out with her," I said. Lee shot me a threatening glance. I threw my hands in the air. "Now it's a business partnership. I won't blend those lines. Not since Reno." I shivered just thinking about it.

"What happened in Reno?" Lee asked suspiciously

Lizzie walked through the door with a small table and a chair.

"That's a story for another time," I told him.

Lizzie unfolded the table and chair and went back inside. She told Lee to hose off Aiko's hands. Aiko giggled as Lee would splash her. Lizzie laughed seeing them when she walked out with a pitcher of lemonade and some cups. A moment later, she returned with a plastic green kid's plate and ceramic one.

She sat in the chair Lee had been sitting in and said, "Shepherd's pie tonight. I added extra cream cheese to the potatoes for Fatty. You two are serving yourself."

"Fine, but that's coming out of your tip," I said. She glared at me.

Lee and I went inside to get our plates. He grunted in disgust at the helping I served myself. We got back on the patio to find Keira standing at the base of the patio. She looked down at the ground as Lizzie finished scolding her.

"Ah, another hustler's here to eat my food," Lee exclaimed as he sat in the other rocker.

The glow of the setting sun glowed around her hair like a halo. Her eyes looked down at the faux wood of the patio.

"Now go get some food," Lizzie finished.

I sat down on the steps of the patio and started digging in. I'd finished a quarter of my plate when Keira sat next to me.

She nudged my shoulder. "Is she still looking at me?" she asked.

I looked back. Lizzie smiled at me and nodded.

"Yep, she's scowling at you pretty bad," I said.

"Well, I guess I deserve it."

"Rule number one of this kind of life: never apologize for this kind of life," I said.

"Isn't it dishonest, though?"

"Do people in commercials really get happier when they use whatever product they're pushing?"

"I guess not," she said, pushing her potatoes around with her fork.

"So just treat me like your commercial actor. We'll even do some public workouts you can invite some people to. What do you think about that?"

She looked at me with a smile. "I guess we could do that. In fact, yes, that sounds like a good plan."

"See, we're not dishonest. We're marketers," I said, thinking of Seth Godin's book, *All Marketers Are Liars*. I'd never read it; I just liked the title.

She took a bite and looked out at the setting sun. "They picked a nice plot of land."

The thought of picking out a house with her flashed through my mind. I didn't know where that had come from, so I quickly reminded myself of Reno. Clearing my throat, I tried to push the thought of her away. "We're going to be good business partners," I said to remind myself more than to say anything to her.

"As long as you promise to be honest with me, no matter what."

I put my fork down and extended my hand. "Honesty pact."

She took my hand to shake on it again. Her eyes sparkled in the setting sun, sending a chill down my spine.

"Reno," I whispered to remind myself.

"What was that?" she asked.

"Oh, uh," I stammered. I looked at the ground. "Nothing important." But it was important to remember.

Chapter 6

Things looked good for me in the gym of Snowflake High School at first. A large steel scale had been placed over the wolf, or *lobo*, at the center of the gym. The hardwood floors gleamed. The bleachers had been set up on one side of the gym.

I counted forty other people who looked like they were signing up. Keira and I sat in the bleachers observing them. Her foot bounced up and down. She wore yoga pants and a blue Nike hoodie, and her hair was up in some sort of weird cone bun.

"Relax. Things are looking good for us," I said, leaning back on the bleacher behind me. My hands rested in my blue gym shorts. I wore a white undershirt with a smear of pizza grease on my belly.

"What do you mean?" she whispered. I assumed she thought whispering would keep our secret.

"Look, most of the people in here are women. What do I have that women don't?"

"That's disgusting," she said.

"What? Oh, no, that's not what I meant." I paused. "Although it's related. Anyway, I get to use my natural fountain of testosterone."

"Right." She probably remembered that fat loss in men is a little easier due to our hormones.

"I am worried about that kid over there." I pointed to a large kid with thick curly hair. He leaned against the wall under the basketball hoop.

"Why?"

"In the testosterone game, if I'm a fountain, he's a waterfall. Even so, normally teenagers would be easy to beat. They're lazy. But he had some kids following him with a GoPro, and he keeps talking into his phone. If he's vlogging his weight loss, then he's going to have a ton of encouragement. What do millennials love more than video games?"

"I don't know," she whispered.

"Someone following them around affirming everything they do."

"Oh," she giggled.

"Nothing we can't handle," I said, nudging her with my elbow.

Microphone feedback blared through the gym. We all covered our ears. A man and a woman stood at a microphone next to the scale.

"Hello everyone," the skinny man said. He had thinning gray hair and wore slacks and a golf shirt. "I'm Ron Flake, the president of the Snowflake-Taylor chamber of commerce."

"And I'm Gina Hatch," followed a short woman with brown hair who had to angle the mike down to her. "I'm president of the *Taylor*-Snowflake Fitness Association." Everyone laughed at how she put Taylor first.

"I don't get it," I said to Keira.

"You'd have to live here."

I fished out my driver's license and showed it to her. "I do."

Keira rolled her eyes. "Pay attention," she hissed.

I'd find out later about the rivalry between the two towns. Taylor was much smaller, but it had the Wal-Mart. Snowflake, being larger, had most everything else.

"We're glad to welcome you tonight to our first ever weight loss competition," the man said. "Think *Biggest Loser* meets . . . I don't know. Let's just get healthy. Gina will give us the rules."

"That's right, we're so excited to kick this off tonight. Now, the rules are simple. We're not measuring for the most weight lost. We're looking for the biggest *percentage* of body fat lost. We'll have a weigh-in tonight and one at the halfway point in the middle of October, with the final weigh-in on November fifteenth. We are so excited to get you to establish good healthy goals right as the holidays set in. So many people think they can just start right on the first day of the New Year. Well, let's kick-start good habits sooner! Now, the way wrestlers cut weight is prohibited. No saunas and skipping meals for you." Someone cheered. "That's why we're ending with the muddy obstacle course that's open to everyone. Only those of you who finish are allowed to weigh in. So you'll have to hydrate and eat to compete."

People clapped when she ended.

"That's clever," I murmured to Keira. "Because that's exactly how I would have done it. That's how I got third in a Tampa competition."

Gina continued. "Now, we're going to start the weigh-in right now. We'll measure your waist, and then have you step on the scale. Our biggest donor for the cash prize is First Street Fat Loss and its owner, Reggie Reynolds!" The crowd erupted in applause.

"That's the jerk I told you about."

"Biggest donor?" I asked with a raised eyebrow. A red flag went up in my mind.

"Yeah, why?"

The lights dimmed and a man in a workout suit entered the gym. He had clean-cut black hair. He was short and had a huge smile as he walked through the gym. People cheered like he was some sort of rock star. Only Keira and I didn't applaud.

"Well, hey, gang," he said with a slight drawl. The lights turned back on as he continued. "I'm so excited to be a part of this. I believe so strongly in setting good habits now. Don't get me wrong: I really like the January first resolutions. They are a nice bump to my bottom line at the beginning of every year." The crowd chuckled. "But my conundrum is that I'm in the business of serving you. It's not just about money to me. That's why I've donated five thousand dollars to the prize money!"

Everyone cheered for him again.

"I want to introduce my current project. Come on out, Marty! As he makes his way to the scale, I want to tell you a little bit about Marty Jenkins. Marty recently moved here from Baton Rouge. He was going to be a game warden for the state. Unfortunately, state budget cuts made him lose his job after only a week." The crowd let out a collective sympathetic sigh. "Marty had to live on his savings. We all know what that means, right?" Nobody answered. He frowned a little. "That meant buying cheap, crappy food. In just a month, he gained fifty pounds."

A man walked out from behind the bleachers. He had long, dark hair and a thick beard. His belly bounced as he walked. He looked up at the bleachers with sad brown eyes.

"Well, *I* found Marty when he was so low. I snatched his hand right as he grabbed a bag of Cheetos. I took him under my wing and haven't let him go! He currently works at the front counter of First Street Fat Loss. I'm going to sponsor his education in personal training. Together we're going to turn things around for him!" Reggie lifted Marty's hand in the air.

Everyone cheered, but I had to stare at Marty because something looked familiar.

The chamber of commerce guy took the mic from Reggie. "Thanks, Reggie. I hope we're all inspired by Marty. Well, since you're up here, why don't you step on the scale?"

Marty pulled his long hair back to tie it in a ponytail. That's when it hit me.

"Oh no," I said, bringing my hands to my face. "No, no, no, no, no."

"What?" Keira looked concerned, and she should have been.

My hands were still over my mouth. "That's Kenny Blake!" I moaned.

"Who?" Her hand grabbed my arm when she asked.

"No one really knows his real name. That's what we all know him as in the underground." My hands still covered my mouth. "That guy is probably the best weight-loss ringer in the country."

"A what?"

"This sort of competition isn't unique. Last year, YourTime fitness had a seventy-thousand-dollar competition. They're a small-time franchise gym. There are only about forty across New England. They didn't have seventy grand to give away. So, since they wouldn't want to pay that out, they hired Kenny Blake to win. He gets something; no one really knows what, and the company saves money. I wonder what his angle is? This is small pond stuff. Why is he here?"

Keira gasped. "Someone should say something!"

My mouth fell open looking at her. "Sis, *you* contracted someone like that." I pointed my thumb at myself. Her eyes went wide, and then she slouched.

"So what does this mean to us?" Keira stared down at Reggie.

"We're probably done, sis," I replied, covering my mouth again.

Someone walked down the bleachers cursing. "Stupid Kenny Blake ruins every chance I get." A chunky woman walked past us and right out of the gym.

"I guess she knows," I said, wincing at Keira. "Well sis, I think this one's over already. If I leave tonight I can probably make it to the Debaca County Fair in New Mexico. They're always good for some sort of money prize. Even if it's only a hundred bucks in a cow pie-throwing contest. I need to try to break even for this trip." I stood up to go, but Keira reached out and grabbed my hand. She yanked me back to my seat.

"No. This has to happen," she whispered through gritted teeth.

"No, this can't happen," I whispered back.

"But how can I—?"

I cut her off. "Look. With Fat Blake down there, Reggie has this in the bag. I think you're going to need to find somewhere else to open up shop."

"You don't understand," she pleaded. I looked down at her blue eyes, welling with tears. Women had accused me of being heartless before. I described myself as calculating. There had to be a benefit to the cost of being wherever I was. As soon as I'd seen Kenny, I'd known that I had stumbled into a losing venture. She looked at me with those big eyes. To my horror, something twisted in my chest.

"Bah," I grunted. "Look, you have to bring your A-game. Forget all this crap you learned about setting a pace. You have to develop something good starting the moment I'm off that scale. I mean you have to watch my food intake, my exercise, and my sleep schedule. There's a lot of work you're going to have to do to get me trimmed up. You basically have to be my nagging wife for the next two and a half months. It's rumored that Kenny has a Ph.D. in nutrition. He knows what he's doing."

She smiled. "Deal," she said, throwing her arms around me. My heart fluttered as I smelled her hair.

We missed how much he weighed as we were talking. That would be simple enough to find out later. The opening ceremony had moved on. Now some woman was on the scale. We waited as three more people were called up.

"Jeremy Higgins," Gina called.

They called the teenager I was worried about. His friends were shouting and hollering as he walked up barefoot and without a shirt. His belly rolls jiggled when he stood on the scale.

"Three hundred pounds!" the fitness president announced, followed by cheering from his friends.

"Phil Carroll, please come down." I muttered profanities the entire way down, knowing I should have skipped town with that other woman.

Gina pulled a tape measure around my belly and then motioned me to go to the scale. "Please step on the scale," she said into the mic. The red numbers flashed up at us, and they confirmed how hard this was going to be.

"Two hundred and forty-one pounds," Gina called out.

My finger went into the air as I walked back toward the bleachers. I calculated the best I could to figure out what I needed to do.

Someone grabbed me and pulled me to sit on the bottom bench.

"Phil Carroll? What's it been? Two, three years?" Kenny Blake sat me down and smiled at me. "Long way from Tampa, isn't it?

"Hi, Ken . . . I guess I should call you Marty?"

"Yes, please, if you don't mind. Obviously if you say anything, then I'll have say something." He waved his hands as he spoke.

"What brings you to a small armpit like this?" I had been anxious to know. "Your protégé beat the pants off of us in Tampa, but I didn't think you'd come to something this small."

"Yeah, it's not my usual type of watering hole, but this Reggie guy has me set up. I'm in this luxury cabin about a mile out of town. He brings me whatever I want, and the prize money's all mine," he said, punching me in the arm.

"Really? That's not your normal type of gig."

"Well, I'm tired. I'm treating this more like a vacation. Small town—" he looked me up and down "—small competition. What are you going to have to lose, about sixty pounds?" He laughed.

"I *was* thinking that if I lose forty I'll be golden," I said. I bit my lip, staring at the ceiling in amazement that I was staying.

He lightly slapped my cheek. "Look bud, it's all business, but good luck!" Then he got up and walked out laughing.

Leaning back against the bleacher behind me, I was still staring at the ceiling of the gym when Keira's face came into my view. I rolled my eyes.

"This better be worth it," I warned.

She stuck her hand out and helped me up. "It will be," she said. "Let's go grocery shopping." She took me by the arm and led me out the gym.

***

"Mom, I'll try to be back for Thanksgiving," I promised her on the phone that night. Thanksgiving, I thought, definitely. Businesses try to keep their money. Most competitions during Thanksgiving were for lousy gift cards.

"What about Christmas?" she asked.

"You see, people think about their mortality, so that's a golden time to sell life insurance." I tugged at my collar. Christmas was a great time for competitions. Light de-tangling, tree sawing, and gift wrapping, to name a few. I'd once gotten second place at a snowman-building contest, a thousand dollars for building seven snowmen taller than three feet in an hour. The winner made ten, winning three thousand.

"Well, I just want to spend a Christmas with my baby boy," she whined.

"I'll check the schedule to see if I'm close enough for the day." Ah, I hated lying to Mom.

"If your father, God rest him, saw you abandoning your mother on Christmas day…" she went on. I thought it was odd because I could remember a few Christmases when he'd had to run to the grocery store he managed.

"Okay Mom, I'll try everything I can to be back."

Chapter 7

For our first real workout the next day, Keira met me after Lee's morning jiu-jitsu class. She parked her car at the big building with a copper-pointed clock tower close by the Basha's. It stuck out, surrounded by all the old buildings around it.

"We're going for a run," she said, taking off running.

"Fine, lead the way," I said to myself.

We ran down Main Street without saying much. I figured it was about three miles when we finally stopped. I didn't think I was in bad shape, but the morning class and a long run? My legs wobbled when we finally stopped at a park. I found the closest drinking fountain and began sucking in water. She motioned to the empty playground equipment, telling me I had to do a hundred silly-looking push-ups on the steps. Then I finished off by maxing out as many pull-ups on the monkey bars as I could. And that wasn't many. When I caught my breath, she began running back the way we'd come. I grunted in frustration and chased after her.

"So, how do you make your basic money?" Keira asked me as she slowed down a mile from where we'd started. "You can't just live on prize money, right?"

"Amazon, eBay, and other websites," I panted. Why was she running so fast? I thought I could run, but I was in trouble with this workout. Not to mention how much I despised running.

"You sell things?" she asked. I was jealous at how easy it seemed for her to talk and run, while my lungs burned.

"I review things," I said.

"So you're one of those guys who gets free stuff and puts out reviews?"

"I don't really have an actual address, so no," I said between gulps of air.

"You do fake reviews?"

"You wouldn't believe—how much people —trust a paragraph by a stranger," I forced between my panting.

We passed by a sign that said we were in Bellybutton, USA. I didn't know what that meant. We began to climb a hill back into Taylor. When we reached the top of the hill, she slowed down more to begin our cool-down jog.

"So you make up reviews for things you have never seen?"

"Remember what I said about marketing? It's really all about polishing trash into a pearl," I wheezed. "We think five stars on a website is good. It's probably just a lie. See that motel up there, the green one? They could be great, but they might be terrible. For a few dollars and in thirty seconds I can make them sound wonderful on Hotel Advisor."

"Do these websites just let you review?"

"Some are smart. They only let you review what you've bought. Others are so general that you can review anything. How do they know I wasn't actually at the motel?"

"That's dishonest."

"It keeps gas in the Bago."

"It's still lying."

"Meh, that's hazy." I shrugged it off. We were in view of her car and it couldn't have looked better.

"How much are your school loans?" I asked, not expecting a reply.

"Seventy thousand," she mumbled.

"Geez, what was the tuition?"

"That's private," she snapped.

"We promised honesty."

"Five hundred and twenty per credit hour and then more for the masters."

"Stop." I hunched over. "I'm sorry, I just threw up in my mouth a little when you said that. You paid how much?"

"The promise is honesty, not repetition," she sneered.

"How much of that was even in stuff you were supposed to learn for this?"

"What do you mean?"

My finger went in the air. "I figure, you had to take two English classes, three credit hours each, two math classes six, a computer class three, a couple of humanities classes six, two history classes six," I said, adding it up in the sky. "That's over twelve thousand dollars. Wait." I looked at her. "That's over twelve thousand dollars on classes you don't need! All so you could take me running?"

"It's called being well rounded."

"Or duped. You want to talk about dishonesty, let's talk about higher education!"

"But college graduates make more money. It's an investment."

"But you have to pay a small mortgage before you start seeing the profit. The cost-benefit analysis doesn't seem to pay off. Now that you graduated, you have to chase down the interest on the loan first. Wait, is that what you are doing? You deferred payment, didn't you?"

"Just run, Fatty," she said when we got to the parking lot. She reached into her Mini Coop and tossed me an apple and a bottle of water. "I'll meet you at your non-graduate mansion at five tonight," she said as she hopped into her car and drove off.

At first I thought it was a good thing she left, because I found the nearest trash can to begin dry heaving. I didn't want her to see me, but I looked up to find three Native American kids pointing and laughing at me. When the last wretch passed and I could stand up straight, I wobbled down the sidewalk of the strip mall to the Sushi Stop. I stumbled inside to the bar and sat next to the bonsai tree.

Lee and his Uncle Tim wore white aprons as they shuffled and spun around each other prepping the sushi station. They juggled cuts of fish, bowls of rice, and vegetables. In one of his passes near me, Tim handed me the scissors to trim the tree. "How about *you* start taking care of that stupid thing?"

"Okay," I muttered, focusing on the small tree. "I think Keira's mad at me."

"Careful, she's fragile," Lee warned me while he chopped carrots and celery. "I've been watching over her for a few years now."

"Yeah, I guess so. I thought she'd be a little tougher. She has a rough exterior."

"Nah, they all need a gentle hand. The bark may seem tough, but the insides are fragile."

I thought of Lizzie. Lee would do anything for her, I thought as I looked out the window at the hick town. Even with all her cursing and demanding, I'd never seen him raise his voice, roll his eyes, or say something mean to her the way I thought I would.

"Plus," Tim added, "if you want them to stick around, you can't cut deep. You conform to their needs, not the other way around. They may not know it, but they are a gift to man to soften our touch."

"You do need a balance though," Lee contested. "It's all about what they need when they need it. Sometimes you really need to rake up some dirt, but keep it gentle so they don't bruise every time you show up."

"Wow, you guys get women way better than I do."

The two of them stopped. They faced me, scrunching their eyebrows. Lee lifted his knife pointing at me. "What are you talking about?"

"Keira."

Lee frowned. "I'm talking about the bonsai, you idiot."

"He thinks we understand women!" Tim chuckled. "Son, there's only one type of man that understands women, and that's only because of his years of training in a certain medical specialty."

"But that was all really good advice," I whined.

"Here's the most important piece of advice when it comes to women." Lee pointed the knife at me again. "Don't listen to anyone's advice on women."

"I taught you well, grasshopper." Tim laughed at himself.

"Thank you, Uncle Sensei." Lee bowed to his uncle. Then they both laughed. Lee set his knife down and pulled a rag from his pocket to wipe his brow. "So, what were you saying? Keira's mad at you?"

"Yeah, I think so."

"Don't worry. She's like her sister. One good stern look will set her straight."

"Really?"

"No. Don't tell Lizzie I said that." Lee and Tim began to laugh again. "Pleading, begging, and groveling does the trick for me. But don't tell Lizzie I said that either."

This time I laughed. I set down the scissors and swept the loose leaves into the palm of my hand. Lee offered a paper towel to drop them on, then he threw them in the trash. My stomach growled, watching them get the food ready.

"So, Lee, buddy, when you headed home?"

"Couple hours, why?"

"You wouldn't, I don't know . . . want to run me home real quick, would you?"

"Hey, go get yourself ahead of the game. Walk home."

My face scowled at him for a moment, but he didn't look up from his work to see me. I shrugged, figuring walking the six miles would probably help burn a few more calories. My stomach rumbled again when I walked out the door. I needed to walk fast since I couldn't wait to get to the Winnebago to bust open a Lean Cuisine.

***

"Okay, look," I said between heavy breaths the day after Keira left me at the Basha's parking lot. My lungs heaved in and out, having finished a few shuttle runs in the playground near the edge of town. It was time to take Lee's advice about groveling. I collapsed in the sand at her feet. "You're doing a great job. But we're going to have to work on our communication a little here. I'm sorry I made fun of you about the college stuff. Since then you haven't said a word to me other than telling me what to do. I don't know, can we still talk a little? I told you to be my nagging wife, not my drill sergeant." The morning workout had been filled with silence as we ran up and down Lee's road. The workout this afternoon had begun in silence too.

Keira stared down at me with one raised eyebrow. I wore a sweaty dark green shirt. At least I didn't look like the fat teenage kid, Jeremy, with the groupies from the weigh-in. When we got to the park we had found him lying on the sidewalk, panting, with sweat trickling off his forehead. One of his buddies had fanned him with a big towel while another filmed the whole thing. They'd helped him climb into the back of a truck and taken off before we'd started working out.

"What do you want to hear?" she asked me with a stern face. "No more lectures about finances?"

"I promise not to bring it back up." I pulled myself back to my feet, sand sprinkling off of me. "I don't know, what do you really like to do for fun?"

"Run two more drills and I'll tell you." She shooed me away.

I took off. When I finished, I collapsed on the small self-propelled merry-go-round. I lay back, putting my head in the center of the steel spinner. My lungs heaved in and out in the thin plateau air that I was still getting used to.

Keira sat down next to me, moving the merry-go-round back and forth. "I don't really know what I like," she gently admitted, staring at the sand.

"How can you not know what you like?" I asked.

"I just—I don't know."

"I don't understand. Isn't there something that has gotten your heart going? If someone made you stop doing that thing, you'd think it were a punishment?"

"Not everyone can travel across the country doing whatever they want."

"That's not what I like. The traveling gets kind of old sometimes."

She looked back at me, wrinkling her forehead. "Why do you do it?"

I thought a moment. "I don't have anything else."

Her eyebrows furrowed. "What else would you do?"

"I'd do what Lee does."

"Own a sushi place?"

I thought about it. "I guess that wouldn't be so bad, if I knew how to roll raw fish. But I've only ever really wanted to teach jiu-jitsu and run my own school. You know, be like a samurai or something when I grow up."

Keira shot me a confused glance. "So why don't you? Do you still train?"

"Yeah, I've always tried dropping in at random gyms around the country. But it's not that simple. I got banned from the real system I believe in."

"For that whole Lee and Lizzie thing?"

"Yeah. I tried to convince Flip, the guy that developed our system, that we needed to stack a weight class at a tournament with mostly his students. The guy has revolutionized the sport with some new theories and techniques he developed. If any of us faced other students, we could take our time. We'd each show the audience his techniques."

"But if I understand the story, he didn't quite agree with your style of...marketing?"

I sat up next to her. "That is the way that I would put it, yes."

"Oh."

"So, Lee had finally convinced this bombshell that he fell in love with to come see a tournament. We both made it to the finals. So I told Lee I'd give him the win and we'd make it look like a real battle. Well, we went back and forth with all the stuff Flip invented. There were twenty seconds left in the match. I let Lee use one of Flip's signature transitions into a triangle choke.

"Everyone thought it was the best match they had ever seen. Except Flip, he knew us too well. He took us both out back and tore into us. He banned us from any of his affiliate gyms and sent us packing. It was the last straw. So I quit school, packed what I needed, and tossed my apartment keys to the landlord."

A shadow of a big cloud floated over us, blocking the sun. Keira picked up a rock and threw it into the sand. I lay back down to watch the clouds floating and mutating. She followed suit, and we watched them together. Her head rested close to mine, and I wanted to turn and watch her. *Reno*, I told myself.

"What were the other straws?" she asked as she pointed in the air and her finger started outlining the cloud.

"Other straws?" I asked, looking over at her.

"You said being banned was the last straw. What were the other ones?"

"Oh," I said, watching her finger. "Well I had a scholarship to Cal-Riverside. I like numbers. I like watching money. The problem was, I worked as a teller for Wells Fargo earning nine-fifty an hour. Sure, once I got my degree I could have made a whole lot more. But people would come in and give me their money. I did the math once. In the one hour that I made nine dollars and fifty cents, I had processed over ten thousand dollars in deposits. Granted, I wasn't the reason they were bringing money in. I just hated the fact that all the math and accounting stuff I had learned to that point would only be used to count other people's money. I don't know about you, but I just want to count my own money. I hoped I could take my degree and apply the principles to a gym of my own."

I took a deep breath then slowly exhaled, my lips quivering a little. "Just after Christmas my senior year of high school, my dad died of a heart attack in his grocery store." I felt Keira turn to look at me. "He ran that place with dedication. I don't blame him for all the time he put into it. It was a good job and he was good at it. When he died, we got a letter from the chain reminding us that we couldn't sue them. I didn't expect them to give us a million dollars. His life insurance covered our needs. But receiving a letter that said, 'you can't sue' didn't help me ever want to work for anyone else.

"So now I go around worrying about my money *my* way. It takes blatantly lying to my mom, but she'd lose it if she found out I'm not a life insurance salesman. Or that I didn't actually get a degree."

She continued looking at me, and I studied her face. We didn't say anything for a moment.

"So, you really can't do what you want?" she asked.

"Right. I'm happy it worked out for Lee, but I really shot my own foot." I pulled myself up to run again. "No time to be a victim. We should get back to . . . ." I stopped. Kenny and Reggie were walking toward us through the sand. "Crap."

Keira got up and saw them too. She turned to me. "Should we leave?"

It was too late. "What's happening, team?" Reggie greeted us with handshakes.

Kenny and I just looked at each other. "Phil," he said, acknowledging my presence.

"Marty," I said.

Reggie just laughed. "No pretense necessary. I assume we all know what's truly going on?"

We all looked at Keira, who nodded.

"Like I thought," Reggie said. "Let's go sit and talk." He pointed to the covered picnic area.

Reggie and Kenny led the way. Reggie wore a running suit with the name of his gym, First Street Fat Loss, on the back. Kenny appeared completely different. He had buzzed his head and shaved his face. His thick eyebrows were the only things that stood out.

Keira and I sat across from our opponents.

Kenny pulled out a bag of celery and held one out to me. "Would you like a snack, Carroll?"

I looked him right in the eyes. "No thanks, I just had some water." He smirked at that.

"So, what do you want?" Keira asked.

"It's no secret what I want." Reggie smiled wide. "I want to crush you. I can charge sixty dollars an hour without ants like you up here."

"Ants?" Keira gritted her teeth.

"Yes. Look. I realize that if I lived in L.A. I'd be some small fish. But here, I *am* fitness. The 'Taylor-Snowflake Fitness Alliance'?" he did air quotes. "That's me. There are a couple of doctors and nutritionists involved, but they all refer their clients to you know who. If *you* share the market, *I* have to lower my prices. I don't want to do that. This whole competition is about proving that. So I have a proposal." Reggie looked at her. Keira looked away and he smiled.

"Go on," I said.

"I've done the math, Miss Brimhall. You don't have a gym. By the looks of that tiny car of yours, you don't have mobile equipment. My first guess was that you got a three-hundred-dollar personal trainer certificate. Reggie assures me you wouldn't have brought in a ringer like Mr. Carroll with only a stupid certificate. So—and correct me if I'm wrong—you probably have a degree in Phys Ed or something that you are still paying off? Meaning you thought you'd take home the trainer winnings?" I bit my lip and Keira's face went red. "That's it, isn't it? Look, I'm not in this for the prize money. Like I said, you all are ants. I've got the facility, I've got the experience, and I've got the best fat ringer in the country."

"I still haven't beaten Vasily Kruchev, or he'd say the world," Blake laughed.

"So I have an offer for you."

Keira dropped her gaze to the cement tabletop. Reggie waited for her to look up. "I'll give you each a thousand dollars to quit."

I couldn't help but whistle. My finger jumped in the air, calculating numbers. With what I'd spent to get to the Podunk town, a grand at that point was just enough to turn a couple hundred dollars in profit. When I finished my math I looked over at Keira's eyes. Her soft sparkles had disappeared, transforming into a fierce glare. The muscles of her cheeks strained, and I imagined her teeth grinding.

"No," she whispered, looking at me.

"Miss Brimhall?" Reggie began. "A thousand bucks is a good start-up. You can take that down the hill to Payson or west Prescott. Heck, I'm sure the Navajo up in Holbrook could drop a few pounds. That would go a long way up there."

"No." She pounded the table.

"Whoa, no need to lose your temper." Reggie smiled through his perfect white teeth. "Just think about it. Call the gym at any time and let me know."

Reggie extended his hand, but Keira wouldn't look him in the eye, ignoring the gesture.

Kenny got up and sauntered over to me, crunching on his celery. "Just my hair weighed three pounds."

"Don't forget those eyebrows, at least another pound right there."

He frowned and followed Reggie over to a new red Ford Mustang. They zoomed out of the parking lot. Keira sat silently at the table.

"Are you okay?" I asked her.

"We *have* to win." She smacked the table again.

I backed up a step. "I don't know, maybe he's right?"

"He is right." She rolled her eyes. "That's not the point." Keira jumped to her feet and began pacing back and forth. I sat to watch her.

"So . . . you want to explain to me what the point is?"

"This is my home." She looked around. "This is where I want to build my life."

I looked around. It wasn't an ugly town. I liked the western feel of the bluffs, the tractors, and the American flags down Main Street. I couldn't believe it was really worth fighting for, though. I had passed through hundreds of towns just like this one.

"Sis, look. He has the advantage in every way. You really want to put down roots in a town where the majority of the houses are mobile?"

"That's because of the clay deposits in the ground, okay?"

"Honesty pact?"

Keira nodded.

"What's keeping you here?"

She bit her lower lip, taking a deep breath. "I'll show you."

I followed Keira to her car. She drove us through town, by the rodeo grounds, and into a cemetery.

"Not where I was expecting you'd take us," I mumbled.

Keira shushed me and got out of the car. I followed her past a set of headstones. One large pinkish stone with two names, Jack and Belinda Brimhall, looked up at us. Some square building was etched between their names.

"Meet my mom and dad." Keira shrugged, staring at the headstone.

"Oh. Okay?" I softly kicked the ground.

Keira turned to me. Her eyes began welling up. "This is home." Then she pointed down the row of headstones. I finally noticed that all of them had the name Brimhall, down to the small, ancient-looking ones.

I shook my head. I'd thought I would do anything for her looking into her eyes when she was happy. Now, with a tear rolling down her cheek, I wanted to do what it took to make her happy again. In my experience, emotional decisions lost me money. But looking down at her, watching another tear fall, all I could say was, "Okay."

My chest fluttered when she looped her arm around mine and led me back to her car.

Chapter 8

The sudden drop in calories and increased activity took a devastating toll that Friday morning after the weigh-in. I could barely keep my eyes alert when I opened my door. Keira bounced up and down in the grass while I dragged my feet to meet her.

"You ready for a run? Why do you look like you just finished the Bataan Death March?"

"First, I'm surprised you pulled out a historical reference. Second, really? On the lawn of a Japanese guy?"

"I minored in history."

My exhaustion passed for a moment. "A minor in history but a major in … health … something?"

"Kinese … sure. Health something works. Ready to run?"

"Yeah, let's do this."

My feet thudded through gravel road following the light tap of her steps. Just ahead, where the gravel met the asphalt, we saw the flashing lights of a black SUV with the blue word POLICE across the hood. The door popped open and a G.I. Joe-type officer stepped onto the road. He had a veiny neck bigger than my thigh.

"Uh, hey, Keira."

"Jeff, what's up? What's with the lights?"

"So, it's against city code to jog on city streets."

"We're barely in town."

"I know, but the city maintains this part of the road. About two miles out it's county road and you'll be okay. You just have to jog on the shoulder or sidewalk."

"Tim, look at the shoulder. It's a gravel slope into sagebrush. We can't run in that. And we're two miles from the nearest sidewalk."

"K, look, I'm sorry. It's the law . . . and—"

"And what?" Keira folded her arms and squared her shoulders.

"Reggie wanted me to make sure you knew he was the concerned citizen making the complaint about joggers out here."

Keira's eyes widened.

"Jeff! You took me to prom!"

"Yeah, but Reggie helped my wife lose, like, a bunch of weight. She's more active, more confident . . . he called me to return the favor. I'm sorry, but he's technically right. You can't be running on the road out here."

Policeman Jeff spun on his heel then jumped back into the SUV. The passenger side window rolled down. "You guys need a ride back to Lizzie's?" he called. Keira shot a look warning him off.

We ran back to Lizzie and Lee's, where she ordered me into her car. Rocks kicked in the air when she shot forward. Of all the forms of Keira I had met—sad, scheming, happy, and perturbed—angry Keira was the most frightening, and a little sexy. Mostly frightening. She didn't slow for the turn when we boomeranged onto Main Street. A pedestrian jumped back onto the curb when she skidded turning toward the rodeo grounds. My head shot forward when she slammed on the brakes near the entrance.

"We'll do bleachers here," she growled.

"Yes, ma'am," I mumbled in fear.

Walking up the ramp to the bleachers, we found a cowboy leaning against the metal railing. He slouched, holding his hat in front of him with both hands. The cowboy glanced at Keira, then stared down at the ground.

"Hey, Miss Keira."

"Miss? Freddy, you used to date Lizzie. You drove us to stake dances."

"So . . . one of my sponsors reminded me of the Parks and Rec rules about being in the bleachers."

"What rules?" I saw Keira's face go red and decided to do the talking.

"The bleachers are only open during events. Insurance reasons," Cowboy said, looking down.

Keira's fists clenched. That's when I saw the giant First Street Fat Loss sign under the announcer box.

"Sponsor?" I pointed to the sign.

"Look, Keira. Remember two years ago when the bull stepped on my back? There wasn't anywhere close by to do real physical therapy. Reggie let my therapist work with me at his gym. The only cost was that sign. I'm awfully sorry, Miss—I mean, Keira."

Freddy the cowboy placed his hat on his head, brushed past us, then walked toward a pen filled with calves. Keira marched toward the bleachers, regardless of the rules. On the first row she sat, dropping her head in her hands.

I sat next to her, holding my breath until I figured out how to say it to her. "I think we need to call Reggie."

"Of course we do," she groaned.

"So . . . ?"

"Can you make the call?" She held out a pink iPhone.

I held down the button until the ding. "Siri? Call First Street Fat Loss."

Siri obliged. While it rang, Keira leaned against me, resting her head on my arm. A shock jolted through my body. I had to think of Reno again.

"First Street Fat Loss, this is Marty."

"Ha!" I shook my head. "Marty?"

"Yes, how may I help you?"

"Well Marty, this is Phil Carroll. I'd like to speak with Reggie, please."

"Well hello, Mr. Carroll. Reggie has been waiting for your call. Let me transfer you to him now."

I hit the speaker button. Without much of a pause, Reggie's voice called through the phone. "Philly boy! I've been waiting to hear from you and Mademoiselle Brimhall!"

Keira's jaws clenched against my arm at that.

"I'm sure you have—"

"Why don't you two come on over to ol' Snowflake for a chat. I just made a fresh batch of gluten-free granola!"

"Fine, we're on our way."

Keira pulled her head away from my arm to look up at me.

"Guess we're headed to Snowflake."

"I'll pull out my recommend."

"Your what?"

"Nothing. Let's go."

Her anger had vanished. Defeated Keira dragged her feet to her car with fallen shoulders. She drove slower this time down Main Street. The only spark of life was when she sneered at the "Welcome to Snowflake" sign.

"Why do you hate Snowflake?"

"I guess I don't *hate* Snowflake. I went to high school here; half my cousins live here; everyone in Taylor has some sort of connection to Snowflake. They just like reminding us where they're from. The old story is that all the families that settled Taylor first started settling the Snowflake area. The Flake family moved in, bought a whole bunch of land, and forced most everyone out. So they moved up the creek to settle Taylor. The Flakes named the town Snowflake after themselves and the prophet at the time. So eventually the families in Taylor, not to be one-upped, named their town Taylor, after another prophet. So there's been a small rivalry as long as I can remember. The creek runs through Taylor into Snowflake. My dad used to say he'd pee in the creek knowing the Flake boys would swim in it. My grandpa taught me this poem: 'Here's to dear old Snowflake, where my ancestors tilled the sod. Where the Smiths only talk to Flakes, and the Flakes only talk to God.'"

I couldn't help but laugh at that, and Keira eventually joined in. Maybe this town had a little more personality than I'd thought. Peeing in the creek and making up poems?

We turned onto First Street to find what looked like a car mechanic shop with big roll-up doors with windows. After getting out of the car, we walked through an open metal door where you'd expect to turn in a set of keys.

Marty smiled at seeing us. "Hello! Can I interest you in a membership? Our couples' membership is discounted and gets both of you in at any time. My shift is up in an hour, so if you do it now we'll make sure I get credit for it."

"Hey, slim. Just point us to Reggie."

"Straight through the gym, the office in the corner. Have a great day!"

We stepped through another door into what used to be the mechanic bays. Stiff rubber mats covered the ground and exercise machines lined the walls. The center of the gym was clear except for a group of about fifteen women in a circle doing squats with their hands behind their heads. A cute redhead in a purple gym shirt and yoga pants led their workout. We walked to the gray metal door with a manager plaque next to it.

After knocking, we heard a muted "Enter!" order us in. We walked in to find Reggie with his hands behind his head and his feet on the desk in front of him. His perfect white teeth glowed under the ceiling lights. Behind him was a canvas photo of someone tanned and greased striking a bodybuilding pose.

"Hey, team! Come on in, get comfortable."

We both looked at the one chair opposite his desk.

"Keira, have a seat. Phil, I'll have Marty bring one for you." Reggie hit his phone. "Marty, please come on back here. Bring Phil a . . . seat."

While we waited, Reggie just kept flashing his smile at us. I looked more closely at the picture behind him. I cringed when it dawned on me that it was a picture of him. Finally, Blake opened the door, rolling in an exercise balloon ball, and leaned against the door. I stood looking at it, wondering why he'd brought it. He pointed to it with his lips and raised his eyebrows.

"Oh, I get it," I said. "A seat." The ball rubbed against my leg, making a small fart noise when I sat.

"Great. Everyone comfortable?" Reggie didn't wait for a reply but slid open a drawer and pulled out a Ziploc bag filled with granola. "Hungry, Phil?"

I just shook my head.

"So, have you thought about my offer? One thousand dollars for each of you is still on the table."

I wanted to remain still and silent since this was going to be her fight. Keira's face remained expressionless as she shook her head.

"So what do we do, sister Sue? You've seen my castle. You've met my minion. What is it you think you can accomplish?"

Keira bit her lip. To me it seemed that the bodybuilding picture of Reggie was laughing down at me. I perked up when I remembered the BattleFrog shirt that Keira had worn. The ball rubbed again when I leaned in to Keira. I covered her ear and whispered, "Challenge him."

She brought her head away to look at me with a confused scowl. I gestured for her to come back.

"Look up there. Let's play on his image. Challenge him to race you."

Keira smiled when she got it. "Reggie, what if we leave the decision up to the race?"

He frowned. "The race?"

"Yeah," I interrupted. "Who cares what happens between me and Blake? If everyone sees you win, wouldn't that be enough?"

He brought his hand up to rub his chin. "So . . . when I win, you, what? Leave town?"

"Uh . . ." Keira hesitated.

"Yep, all or nothing for her. And for you, I think splitting the two towns sounds great, right?"

Both Keira and Reggie looked at me in amazement. Keira's fingers turned white gripping the arm of the chair. Reggie kept rubbing his chin.

"I mean, *if* you can beat her."

"That's not going to work." He scowled at me.

"What, watching you lose to someone from Taylor?" I said out of the side of my mouth. "My competition will not change with Kenny." Kenny smiled at that. He put one palm up and started rubbing his other hand over it like he was "making it rain" dollar bills. "You gave a bull rider a place to do his therapy, so I believe you're a fair guy. This competition will come down to Kenny and me. Eventually the two of us will leave your rivalry behind. Even if you lose," I said to Keira, "you'll still impress everyone with my weight loss."

Reggie sucked his top lip, thinking about it. "Okay," he growled, slamming his hand on his desk.

"Fine," Keira grunted. "Will you call off your hounds and let us train?"

Reggie lifted his hand in the air. "Of course. Now, I have a race to train for. If you don't mind?" He pointed at the door.

Blake opened the door for us to retreat from Reggie's office. We walked through the gym and out to her car.

"Is anyone looking?" Keira asked. I looked around and back into the gym. No one saw us, so I shook my head.

She jumped at me and I caught her in my arms. Her face was so close to mine. I stared at her lips just inches from mine. I let her fall to her feet and stepped back with a deep breath. *Reno, Reno, Reno*, I thought to myself. Keira bit her lower lip, pumping her fist in the air.

"I thought you were mad at me," I said, putting her back on her feet.

"Nope, this is perfect."

"How's that?"

74

"Mud races," she said with a giggle. "I love them! I was on the NAU BattleFrog team." She paced back and forth excitedly. "I mean, we weren't very good, but I always crushed it. Come on, let's go running!"

I smirked, watching her get in the car.

***

At dinner that night, Lee's eyes got a workout. Almost every time Keira or I said something about the day, he ended up rolling his eyes.

"So cowboy Fred moseys over," I said with a drawl. I turned to Aiko. "Hey, you rascal!" I poked Aiko's side, making her squeal. "Ain't nobody 'llowed on these here bleachers!"

Lee rolled his eyes. Lizzie and Keira laughed with Aiko when I poked her side again. Then I looked down with a frown at the small chicken breast and broccoli that sat on my plate. Aiko had barely touched her fish sticks. I inched my finger toward her plate.

"Uh-uh, pardner," Keira drawled, catching me mid-temptation. "Not while Sheriff Keira's in town." She sat on the other side of Aiko and poked her other side, forcing another round of giggles.

When all the girls looked back at their plates, I felt a kick under the table. I looked over to find Lee mouthing at me to *stop flirting*. I just shrugged.

"So to celebrate our first week, I'm taking Phil to Eva's tomorrow."

"Celebrating the week with fried Mexican food?" Lee asked with another roll of the eyes.

"Eva's daughter, Manuela, and I go way back." Keira pointed a fork full of chicken at Lee. "She'll whip up something light and healthy for Old Philly Boy here."

She used the nickname Reggie had used when I'd called him.

"Where's Eva's?" I asked.

"Just a couple of blocks from Reggie's gym," Lizzie said.

"Snowflake? I thought we avoided Snowflake."

"When possible," Lizzie said before spooning some coleslaw into her mouth. "But," she went on after swallowing, "Eva's doesn't count. Eva's is neutral."

"Ah, dear old Snowflake, where *your* ancestors tilled the sod. Where the Smiths only speak to Flakes, and the Flakes only speak to God," I recited.

Lizzie and Keira laughed wildly at my rendition. Eventually, even Lee joined in, after rolling his eyes one last time.

I looked over at Keira and she looked back at me with that smile.

Chapter 9

"Keira!" a young, plump Mexican girl called when we walked through the door of La Cocina de Eva. "You never come in anymore. Oh, and who is this?" She looked me up and down.

"This is Phil Carroll. He's the one I told you about."

"Right, grilled chicken and extra leafy stuff. The chicken is on the griddle away from all the oils and grease."

"Thanks, Manuela."

"Of course. Follow me. I have the perfect spot."

We followed Manuela through the restaurant lined with wood paneling. As we stepped across the dingy brown carpet, the floorboards beneath creaked us. Manuela sat us at a small table with only two seats beneath a painting of a man on a horse leading a donkey. When we sat, our knees bumped together and she instantly scooted back some. Our fingertips nearly brushed, and I pulled my silverware closer to the edge of the table then folded my arms.

"I guess there's no point in looking at the menu," I mumbled.

"Of course you can look, but our food has already been ordered."

"Great, I guess," I said, rolling my eyes. "Can't wait for more salad."

"It's not that bad. Just smaller servings—you'll be all right."

My stomach growled as I watched a round man shoving forkfuls of chimichanga into his mouth. I frowned in envy, seeing rice spilling down his shirt.

"Stop staring." Keira leaned back in her chair, making the floor creak.

"I can't help it." I looked back at her. She wore a green and blue flannel shirt. The green in the shirt accented the shade of her eyes. I groaned thinking about how beautiful she was, so my eyes drifted back to the shrinking chimichanga. "What's the plan this coming week?" I asked, changing the subject.

"I've asked a, uh, friend to help come up with some workouts for you. So we don't plateau. I want you to keep the weight dropping, and he'll know how to develop a good, scientific program."

"Okay, but isn't that why you went to school, so you can develop a program yourself?"

"Right. But programming for an average person compared to someone trying to win a weight loss competition is a little different."

"Shouldn't it all be related?"

"I guess so—"

"I mean, that's why you went to school, right?" I felt how insensitive that sounded as soon as I said it. "Sorry, that was mean."

Keira's face went red, but just then Manuela saved the day. She arrived with our food, laying down our plates of grilled chicken, bits of corn, and diced tomatoes resting on a bed of spinach. The salad came with some sort of oily dressing. Manuela also placed glasses of water in front of us. After thanking Manuela, we returned to our silence.

"Suffering with me on the salad?" I tried to break the awkward pause.

"Look, I like the exercise world. I'd rather talk about muscles and bones than about anything else. But…"

"But?"

She grimaced.

"Honesty pact," I sang.

"In the end, sometimes I feel like I'm not supposed to be a twenty-nine-year-old Mormon with a divorce under my belt. Like I'm supposed to be at home with a family."

"Who said you're *supposed*—you were married?"

"Yes. And no one really said that, technically. But there's so much emphasis on marriage and motherhood around here."

"You can't do what you want *and* be a good mom? Wait, *are* you a mom?"

"No, I'm not a mom." She bit her lip. "I don't know. I just look at Lizzie and a bunch of other women at church and feel that they do it all better. Good wife, good mom, good sister."

We both looked down at the table and then began to eat. When she had eaten most of the salad and all of the chicken, she put her silverware down.

"Why are you doing all this?" she asked.

"I told you." I munched on the leaves. "I don't have anything else."

"I only buy that . . . to an extent. Don't you have anything planned in the long term?"

"Yeah, one day I'll have to actually stick my feet in the dirt and keep them there."

"And what is going to make you do that?"

"Oh, it's nothing." I took another bite.

"Honesty pact," she sang back to me.

"Fine. It all starts with going to Japan."

"What do you mean?"

"I might have come up with a way to be a samurai when I grow up, like I told you. A few years ago, I had the thought that I could go to Japan and study original jiu-jitsu at the temple where it was developed. Then I could come back and start my own thing." I chomped at another forkful of lettuce. "I almost have enough to get to Okayama." My finger went in the air to calculate the same numbers I'd run through hundreds of times. "I want to save enough to live there for about six months, maybe longer. Then I'll need to fly back. I have to budget it just right to have enough for first and last month, plus more for an additional few months and equipment to get started. That would be ideal."

"Couldn't you just get back in with your old system?"

"I don't know, maybe. I can't count on it. Lee never told me what he had to do, but I'll just control what I can. I can make it to Japan. I can open my own place."

"Must be nice to have a real plan."

"Unless you and I win, it's probably just a pipe dream."

"You could sell the Winnebago," she said, stabbing her salad again.

She jumped a little when I gasped. "Sell the Bago? *Sell* the Bago?"

"You could probably cover the whole trip, a bunch of rent, and all the equipment you need."

"Sell the—where would I live?"

"A house or an apartment?" She took another bite.

"But that's my baby."

"Boys." She rolled her eyes. "So you plan on never living in a building with a foundation?"

"I guess one day I'll have to," I said after swallowing a bite. "I know I need to do something grounding. Something defining. Japan is all I can think of."

"What do you mean by defining?"

"Something extraordinary that sets me apart, or whatever." I mumbled the last part before putting more salad down.

"So, Japan?"

"Surviving a real Asian martial arts master? Becoming as close to a samurai as I could? Not many Americans can claim that. It's something marketable."

"Is that all you think about? Monetizing things?" Her nose twitched.

"For the most part." I shrugged. "Doing things the same way as everyone else leaves you with the same results as everyone else. Right now all this wandering . . . all this traveling and killing myself for small chunks of money is getting old. In samurai terms, I guess I'm really just a—"

"Ronin?" She smiled.

I gasped again. "Do you even know what that means?"

"A masterless samurai?"

I gasped a third time. "How?"

"Lee got me hooked on samurai movies."

"No!"

"Well, not hooked. I'd still rather have a Jane Austen movie in front of me. But when Lee joined the family I sat in on a few samurai-fests."

"I don't believe you. What's your favorite movie?"

The Twilight Samurai.

"Wow." I sat back, looking at her and realizing I didn't know her as well as I thought.

"Like I said, I don't go looking for them. But if one is on, I won't change the channel."

I stared at her for a few seconds before abruptly standing up. "Excuse me." I found the restroom. When I walked in I stepped to the closest sink. Splashing some water on my face, I marveled at Keira. "A girl to watch samurai movies with?" I shook my head. "Get a grip. Keep it professional." I wiped my face and returned to Keira, trying to avoid looking at her the rest of the night.

Chapter 10

That Sunday morning it surprised me and even hurt a little that Keira didn't knock at five thirty. Instead she showed up at seven in her nice Sunday clothes, carrying a plastic orange platter in the shape of a leaf. It carried some wheat toast, egg whites, and blueberries from Lizzie's kitchen. Her chocolate hair had a braid on one side that she'd tied back along one side of her head. She wore a white- and blue-striped dress with red heels. Big red cherry-looking beads, matching her shoes, hung around her neck.

"It's the Sabbath," she said matter of factly when I asked her where she'd been that morning. "Lizzie said you're going to church again." She sat at the table, watching me eat on the couch.

"Ughh. I went last week," I complained, dropping my head.

"Well, church, it's a weekly thing," she laughed.

"Why?" I wondered.

"To help make being Mormon a twenty-four-seven kind of thing."

I just rolled my eyes. The way Lizzie and Keira talked, it was like being a Mormon was part of their identity. Keira stood up and started going through my cupboards. She shuffled through my plates and cups. She meticulously lifted each dish. Her hands swept things aside to really look as deep as she could in my cupboards.

"What are you doing?" I asked between sucking small seeds from the toast out of my teeth. I moved onto the squishy blueberries.

"Just making sure there aren't any bad snacks in here," she said out of the side of her mouth.

"Okay, that's fine. I have nothing to hide," I said, watching her lean against the counter on her tippy toes. Her dress pulled tight around her. *RENO*, I screamed in my head and bit my knuckle. I looked outside. "Keira! I'm a professional. At any other time, you'd find endless supplies of beef jerky, Twinkies, and sour cream and onion Pringles up there. I spent the afternoon before the weigh-in ridding this place out place of anything tasty."

"What about these?" she asked.

I turned to see what she had. Her eyebrows shot up. She smiled like she had caught me with my hand in a cookie jar. In a way she had, since she held a green package of cookies.

"Ha! Open the package!" I demanded.

She lifted the tab that pulled open the top plastic and pulled out a yellow sticky note I'd taped to the inside with a note to myself. It showed how many I could have a day and when. Her face flushed red as she threw them back in the cupboard.

"A package of cookies isn't worth eight grand, sis," I said with a smile.

"Good," she said. She sat at the table, leaning back in the chair. "Is cowboy Phil coming to church today?"

"I learned my lesson last week," I informed her. I couldn't help but feel claustrophobic again.

"What's that?" she asked, dragging out the words with raised eyebrows.

"The more I stick out, the more people treat me like a pet," I said.

"What?" She glared at me.

"Yeah, I bought a white shirt, some Dockers, and a tie in Show Low when I went to get my license. My plan is to fit in and glide through the three hours."

"It's not *that* bad," she said, pursing her lips.

"Have you ever stood out at one of your churches?" I asked.

"Yes, I was a missionary in Taiwan," she said with a triumphant smile.

"Oh, but—"

"No," she snapped. "I was taller than almost everyone, I was white, and I had a big black name badge on my blouse. So yes, I know what you're going through."

"What's in Taiwan? Why would you want to go there?"

"I wanted to serve the Lord. He called me to go to Taiwan; I didn't actually choose to go there."

"Fair enough," I admitted, now not understanding what she meant by "called." "So, what did you do there?"

"Missionaries preach, so I'd go to people's houses with my companion. We would ask people if they would let us teach them about Jesus and the church."

"What if no one let you in?" I asked. I leaned forward, resting my chin in my hand. There was something different about her as she spoke about it. Her eyes sparkled more, she smiled bigger, she spoke more softly, and her hands moved around, helping her speak. I wanted to drink in this new excitement on her face.

"That happened sometimes—well, maybe most of the time. We would just keep going. Ideally, we wanted members of the church to help us. There were times when we just sucked it up. If there was empty time, we filled it talking to random people on the street."

"You Mormons are a bit weird."

"Peculiar?" she asked.

"Yes, that's a better word." I stood up. "Now if you don't mind, I need to get ready."

I followed her to the door to let her out. Lee and Aiko were out in front of the house walking around. Lee had on some nice pants and his white tank top. I watched Keira walk back to the house. Then I saw Lee watching me with a frown. He pounded his fist into his hand and mouthed the word *Reno*. I zipped the blinds closed. He didn't even know what he was talking about. He only brought it up because I'd mentioned it before.

After only fifteen minutes, I'd showered, shaved, and dressed. In another five minutes, we all sat in Lizzie's van on the way to church. Children's music from the church played. Keira and Aiko sang along. Keira didn't sing like a diva, but her voice sure wasn't terrible.

When we walked into their main meeting hall, I quickly sat down as close to the wall as I could. Lizzie followed me along the bench, then Lee and Aiko, and Keira sat along the aisle. People waved to me, but I had strategically located myself so they couldn't crowd me.

"Lee had to do the same thing for awhile," Lizzie whispered. "Now they just know him as the 'dry Mormon," she said with a laugh.

"What's a dry Mormon?" I whispered back.

"Someone who does all the Mormon stuff without ever getting baptized."

I still looked at her with a blank face.

"In water? Baptism?"

"Oh," I said. Then I gave a small courtesy laugh. Mormons use a lot of weird lingo. "Wait, are you making me a dry Mormon too?"

"The plan is to one day make you a wet Mormon," she said, poking me in the rib.

"Oh, at least you're honest. Did you go to Taiwan too?"

"No, I didn't go on a mission."

"I thought everyone had to?"

"The men are strongly encouraged, but the women aren't as much. A lot go, though."

A tall man stood at the microphone. He had blond hair and wore a tan suit.

"Is there a new bishop?" I whispered to Lizzie.

"That's Brother Hatch. He's the bishop's first counselor, and they take turns conducting."

" . . . we have some stake business by our high counselor . . ."

"Ward, bishop, first counselor, high counselor?" Feeling more comfortable with Lizzie, I knew I could ask her anything. "You all talk funny."

"Yeah, there are some weird words. You'll get used to it."

An old man stood at the podium and waited for it to lower. He had a silver comb-over and a baggy face. "Brothers and sisters, the Stake President sends his love . . ."

"What's a stake? What's a stake president? Is it like a cow steak?"

"Shhh," Lee warned me after a few people turned back to see who was talking.

" . . . the single adults are going to have what they are calling a Victory Dance in two weeks. The jazz band from Snowflake High will be providing forties-era big band music. The theme is World War II dress and style. In my day, we just called that a dance." Everyone laughed. "It will be at the Snowflake Social Hall, where they used to always have those types of dances. I know from experience." Everyone laughed again.

"Do you have to laugh at bad jokes too?" I whispered.

"Shhh," Keira hissed.

Lizzie pulled my arm down. "You're taking Keira to that dance!"

Lee and Keira didn't hear what she'd said. They both glared at me, anticipating I'd say something noisy again. So I just shook my head. Lizzie jammed a single knuckle into one of my ribs. I squirmed in pain, but just shook my head again. Then she pinched my arm and I held in a scream.

"Fine," I wheezed out of the side of my mouth. Lizzie sat back against the bench with a pleased look on her face. Then she frowned and her face went bright red. Her hands gripped Lee's leg. His head popped up. Then his shoulders dropped and he stared at the floor. Aiko giggled, pounded Lee's leg and pointed up the row. Keira brought her hand to her mouth. I tried to understand what had caused the disturbance.

Music started playing as the most perfect-looking man I had ever seen walked toward our bench. His long dark hair was parted down the middle. Not ponytail-long, but Civil-War-shaggy long. I say Civil War because he had a handlebar mustache and a goatee like Colonel Sanders. He wore a custom fit dark blue suit with light brown shoes and a matching belt. He had a big smile with perfect teeth. The smile of someone who knows he's attractive. He was also the most intimidating person I had ever seen. He didn't have a neck, just giant shoulders. Even with a suit coat on, his pecs bulged out. His pants wrapped around his quads like Saran Wrap.

I jumped a little, scared when I heard Lizzie let out a growl. The man just smiled at our bench. Keira lifted Aiko onto her lap and scooted down. The man-beast sat next to her. He waved and Lizzie and Lee, who just flashed fake smiles back at him. He lifted a green song book so that Keira could read along. Then put his arm around her.

"Um, who's that?" I whispered to Lizzie.

"Her ex-husband," she muttered. I shot a surprised glance at her. "I'll tell you later," she said through gritted teeth. Lizzie didn't say anything else the rest of the meeting, letting my world spin.

***

The rest of the sacrament meeting I took side glances at Keira and the hulky Civil War character. He had a huge smile sitting next to her. Her lips were barely curled at the side of her mouth. Aiko bounced up and down on his knee with a giant smile. When the meeting ended, Keira and Señor Muscles took Aiko to the kids' room. I don't know where they went after that. Lee and Lizzie were in a foul mood and didn't want to go to class. I joined them on a bright flowery couch in what Lizzie called the foyer. A fake ficus sat next to me and I played with the velvet leaves.

"That guy's such a jackass," Lizzie said to no one in particular.

"Why would he even be here?" Lee asked, also to no one in particular.

I kept playing with the leaves. "I'm still wondering who this guy is."

"Ryan Hewitt," Lizzie said, grinding her teeth. "All-star Peter Priesthood from down in the valley. When you first meet him, he can do no wrong. My parents probably would have squashed it. They never got to meet him. Only a month after Keira and Ryan met, our parents died in a car accident . . ." her voice trailed off.

"Oh, sorry." Keira hadn't told me how they'd died.

She brushed it off with a shrug. "Well, she tried to fill the hole with Ryan. Those two got married about three months after that. Bam," Lizzie said, snapping. "We were all up here at the temple soon after . . ."

"So, why is he a jackass?"

"He was domineering, critical, a bully to us," Lee listed. "He always told Lizzie and Keira what they could do better."

"I never cooked with the right ingredients. He went on and on one time about the gluten in the noodles I used in my spaghetti. They were just da . . . arn noodles." Lizzie caught herself, looking around at the paintings of Jesus.

"Finally, she couldn't take it anymore and we helped her leave him. We went to Flagstaff to get her and her stuff after she got her bachelor's. She lived with us for a while until she moved in with her current roommates a few blocks away, where she started her online program," Lizzie said. "He stops by sometimes, and every time they try to work it out and every time she starts falling for it again."

Lee nodded. "He's her kryptonite. I mean, yeah, he's hot . . ."

"Yeah," Lizzie said.

That perturbed Lee and he didn't finish his sentence.

I personally had wanted to punch the guy as soon as I'd seen his perfect jaw line. The list of faults Lee had gone over helped me not like him. The way that Keira had looked like she liked his arm around her shoulder drove me crazy. Even though it wasn't any of my business, I felt like it should have been.

DON'T BLUR THE LINE! RENO! I screamed at myself as I fiddled with the leaves.

"You're taking her to that dance," Lizzie ordered me.

"Not now," I informed her.

"Then find a new driveway!" she demanded as she stood up and walked away.

"Babe, where you goin'?" Lee asked.

"To find that stupid girl," she almost yelled.

Lee jumped up to follow her. "Just take her to the dance, please."

I sat thinking about it as the velvet leaf twirled in my finger. That's when the missionaries found me. They plopped down next to me on the couch. One was short with a hawk nose and thick glasses. The other had red hair and freckles.

"Hi, Phil, I'm Elder Thompson," the redhead told me.

"And I'm Elder Baldini," the other said. "We heard you're doing that weight loss thing. What kind of exercising are you doing?"

"Oh, Keira Brimhall is my personal trainer, so I'm just doing whatever she tells me to."

"Who's that guy with Sister Brimhall?" Elder Thompson said.

"I couldn't tell you," I mumbled.

"Well, if you ever want to go bike riding with us, you're more than welcome. We head out about five thirty and go a couple of miles up Pinedale Road and back to our apartment."

"Oh, guys . . ." I had to think of an excuse. "I . . . uh . . . don't have a bike, so I couldn't come."

"That's not a problem," said Elder Baldini. "There's an extra bike at our place we could bring by at any time."

"Oh, well," I stuttered. The little Mormon had stumped me. "Let me run it by Keira—er, Sister Brimhall, I mean, and I'll get back to you."

The redhead pulled out some sort of pocket calendar and tore out a piece of paper and wrote on it. He handed it to me and I saw a phone number. "Call us when you know," he said. They stood up to walk away.

"Are you boys just doing this to get me baptized?" I asked, remembering the words Lizzie and I had gone over in the big meeting.

"Of course," Elder Thompson said with a smile.

Lee walked around the corner and made me follow him to some class.

***

Lizzie, Lee, Aiko, and I came home to find Keira and Ryan on the rocking chairs. A bright blue open Jeep parked behind my RV. He gave us all hugs and told me how proud he was of the life choice I had made. Obviously, Keira hadn't quite told him the truth. I guess she couldn't trust *him* with an honesty pact. I counted one tally mark for me in the imaginary columns I started keeping. Now I just had to beat charming, handsome, and dreamy, as a woman might call him.

Since he was there, Lizzie felt compelled to feed him. He offered to help, but she wouldn't have it. She grabbed Keira and they donned aprons. The three of us men removed our ties and watched a UFC replay. Normally Lee and I would have been talking about the old days when we'd have fight night viewing parties. Or we'd discuss our favorite fights. That day, the two of us just tolerated Ryan talking about the workouts he'd done with some fighters while he played with Aiko. I watched him make small child-like jokes that had Aiko giggling. Him showing up for Keira was one thing, but moving in on my girl Aiko? That was irritating. So I ignored him. I tried to listen to the whispered tongue-lashing that Lizzie was giving Keira. I couldn't really hear their hissing over Mr. Biceps' stories about the Cross Fit games.

For dinner, Lizzie made a beautiful, tasty pot roast that everyone enjoyed. I had a bowl of spinach with tuna and some Italian dressing. I watched Dr. Square Jaw constantly putting his hand on Keira's shoulder. He also got to eat red meat. What an arrogant jerk. I thought that at some point, Lizzie's knife was either going to bend or cut through her dinner plate. Her fingers were white as she gripped the sharp object. Lee, who usually sat close to his beloved wife, sat an arm's distance away from her.

"Lizzie . . ." Ryan began.

"Elizabeth," she cut him off.

"This is so good," he continued. "I really needed the protein. I did ten reps of one of my max squats yesterday. This meat is a godsend." Without warning, he leaned into Aiko's ear and let out a fart noise. Aiko's mouth exploded open in a laugh, showering her food with chewed-up carrots.

Lizzie looked up in surprise. "Thank you." She squinted in suspicion.

"Have you read about the benefits of grass-fed beef?"

"Ah," she said with a frown. "No Ryan, no I haven't."

Again he leaned into Aiko's ear and let out a fart noise. Lizzie glared at Ryan. Keira smiled at him as he laughed with Aiko.

"I'll find the article I read," he began when he and Aiko stopped laughing. "See, the fat on corn-fed beef really isn't good for us. Cows are really supposed to be eating grass . . ." He went off on a tangent that made Lizzie squeeze her fork, turning her knuckles white again.

I watched the room like a fly on the wall. Lee just stared down at his food and ate fast. He avoided eye contact with everyone. Aiko and Keira hung on Ryan's every word. He moved on to talking about the Cross Fit games he had participated in, again. If you'd have asked him, someone was out to get him. He kept getting something called "no reps," and that's why he only ended up in twelfth.

"Lee," he just kept talking. "Bro, you should come with me next year. The place becomes the center of the fitness universe. All the supplement companies, fitness equipment, workout apparel, you name it. They all set up shop and man, you can get anything, dude. He put his hand to his face to block Lizzie and Keira from reading his lips. "And the ladies? Not too shabby." He spoke out of the side of his mouth. Not that it did anything. Lizzie heard every word. I thought steam would come out of her ears. Keira frowned at the comment too.

"Ah, you know," Lee started. "I'm just a squat, deadlift, and bench kind of a guy. I try to stay more specific to my sport."

"See, those old lifts just aren't functional, bro," Ryan said.

"Really?" Lee dropped his fork and it clattered on the plate. "My four-fifty squat isn't—"

"Ryan?" I interrupted Lee. The man had insulted his wife's cooking, but a man should never insult another man's maximum squat weight.

"What's up, bro?" he said, wrapping his hand around my arm.

I laughed a little with how comfortable he felt fondling me. It was hard to imagine that guy ever kissing Keira. She looked at us—well, mostly at him. "So Cross Fit, is that a speed thing or is it a technique thing? How do you find the balance?"

"Oh, broheim, you have to do the technique just right, then you can speed things up. Then you can end up in the Cross Fit games. Like me." He turned to Aiko again, letting out another fart noise.

I stabbed my fork into the last of my spinach. "That's right, where you got twelfth?"

Lizzie covered her mouth to keep from laughing, and Lee almost snorted. I looked at Keira, who glared at me.

"Yeah, bro. I'm going to be showing you in the morning!" he said, pounding me on the arm.

"Oh!" He'd surprised me. "Is that so?" I asked, now glaring back at Keira. She just raised her eyebrows, challenging me with a smile.

Then I ate my salad in silence. The bro-man just kept rambling on about things like Cross Fit, almond milk, and something called ketosis. I had a hard time following it all. I also grew concerned. His stupid perfect jawline and veiny neck kept Keira captured.

I finished long before everyone else. I had to watch them eat the juicy beef and buttery carrots. Aiko had some food that she didn't touch. I wanted to get her to slide her plate over to me, just to make Keira mad.

"Aiko," I whispered. "Give me some carrots."

"Auntie Keira said I can't," she whispered back.

"But you have to. I'm an adult."

"Auntie Keira said you aren't."

I frowned, defeated. Keira, who'd heard the whole thing, giggled.

When the last fork clattered on the plate, Lizzie looked at her sister. "Keira, you're so kind to do our dishes, too."

Keira looked at Lizzie, then at Ryan, and back at Lizzie. "Fine," she said with furrowed eyebrows.

"Babe, I'll come help," Ryan said, standing up.

I pulled him down. "Nah, bro, I'll help," I said. "I need some weekly planning time with my trainer anyway."

"That's a great idea, bro," he said.

Lee stood, picking up his plate, but Lizzie grabbed him by the arm and sat him back down. "Honey," Lizzie said. "We have company. You can't just abandon me— uh, him." She pointed her chin at Ryan.

"Sweetie," Lee said gritting his teeth. "Sunday dishes is my thing, and I want to show you how much I appreciate your loving service."

Lizzie looked at him with squinted eyes. "Sit the hell down."

"So Lee, when you're squatting . . ." Sergeant Traps began.

I jumped up to grab dishes and left Ryan to annoy Lee. Keira followed me into the kitchen. She put her and Ryan's dishes in the sink. She opened the dishwasher but grimaced, then caught herself from cursing.

"Lizzie left dirty dishes in here, and it's full. What a jerk," she said as she pulled two pairs of yellow gloves from a drawer. She filled one part of the sink with hot water. The other had the faucet lightly pouring. She handed me a pair of gloves and said, "You scrub. I'll rinse and dry."

"Fine."

She slipped an apron on, then faced me with another apron, a pink one with yellow frills down the side.

"Oh no!" I said.

"That's your only shirt, and I don't need you to have an excuse to miss church."

"I could always use my cowboy Phil shirt," I suggested.

"Oh no!" she laughed. She lifted the loop over my head. I looked down at her and realized how much I hated Ryan. I reminded myself of Reno, then quickly turned to the sink and dunked Aiko's plastic plate. I scrubbed it with the green side of a sponge. I handed it to her, and then reached for another plate.

She bumped me with her hip. "What's with you?" she asked. "You're acting weird."

Wiping a plate, I thought about what I would say. "You know our honesty pact?" I finally said.

"Don't start. My ex lending a hand doesn't have anything to do with that."

"Him showing up out of nowhere has everything to do with the pact. But I was just trying to be honest with you," I said calmly.

"Oh. Well, what did you want to say?" she asked, wiping a cup and looking at me.

"That guy's a tool," I said handing her the plate.

"Well, I'm sorry, but that tool is our ticket to victory."

"How?" I asked.

"He's here to help me get ready for the race and get you on a Cross Fit regimen," she said, slamming a cup down on a towel.

"What?" She'd shocked me. So that was why he had shown up. Then I remembered her talking about a "friend" that was going to help her develop a program for me.

"He's certified. In one hour he can help you burn about a thousand calories."

"I can do that at Lee's!" I hissed, so the others wouldn't hear.

"I'm planning for your plateau. You won't end up beefing up like him." I watched her say that with a smile out of the corner of my eye.

"When do I have to start?" I asked.

"Tomorrow morning."

"Oh darn," I said with fake disappointment. I tried snapping, but the rubber fingers of the glove just flicked water in my nose.

"What?" she laughed. Then she wiped the drops of water off me. Some of her perfume wafted into my nose. For a second I forgot what I was going to say.

"See, I had committed to a bike ride with the missionaries tomorrow morning," I lied. I sort of lied. They'd invited me. I only had to call them to make it happen. It didn't make me feel any better for breaking our pact. But the thought of being around Ryan nauseated me so much, I had to put it off.

Keira looked at me, watching my face. "Did you really?" she asked.

"Yeah, I thought it'd be good to mix it up a little." I didn't move my face. "Like you said, avoid a plateau."

"Well okay, I guess," she said and turned back to drying dishes.

I patted my pocket, trying to hear if the paper the missionary had given me was still there. To my relief, I heard it crinkle.

"Are you okay?" Keira asked, looking at me.

"Yeah, just stretching my wrist. Those push-ups you had me doing kind of hurt."

When we finished the dishes we returned the to bro-fest. I turned the corner right in time to watch Lizzie pinch Aiko's leg. She let out a long wail.

"Crap," Lizzie said. "She's getting cranky, I better go lie down with her and put her to sleep."

"Yeah," Lee said, catching on to what Lizzie was doing. "I'm going to run to the restaurant. Just to double check on everyone." He got up and walked straight out the door. But I laughed, knowing that he closed the Sushi Stop on Sundays.

"Thanks Lizzie, it was delicious. I'll send you that article on grass-fed beef," Ryan promised.

"I can't wait!" she said with a big fake smile as she walked toward the hall to the rooms.

"Keira, let's go for a drive!" Ryan proposed, heading for the door.

"Okay," she said, a little too eagerly in my opinion.

Lizzie came back out with a teary Aiko. "Take Phil!"

"But—" I protested.

"Take Phil!" she pointed at me.

"Yeah broseph, hop in. We'll talk about our plans."

"Fine, let me go change my shirt," I said. I ran outside, over the grass, onto the drive, and into my RV. I pulled the paper out of my pocket and dialed the number while I put on a polo.

"Elder! It's Phil Carroll" I reminded him.

"Phil, it's great to hear from you." he said. I didn't know who was speaking, but time was of the essence so I didn't care.

"Great, listen. Sister Brimhall said I could come riding with you tomorrow."

"Sweet, is five thirty at the Akiyamas' house still okay?"

"See you then." I hung up my phone to finish restoring the honesty pact. Now that the bike ride was set, she couldn't accuse me of lying. Then I went outside and climbed in behind Keira and Ryan. He started talking more about taking twelfth at the Cross Fit games.

***

I faithfully called Mom when I got home that night.

"Mom, no, these trips are just business. I don't have time to go looking for girls."

"Well, you know, I'm not getting younger. Sarah Robinson down the street has eight grandchildren now. Eight!"

"Well, Mrs. Robinson had five kids. You just had me," I told her.

"I don't see what that has to do with anything."

I stuck my finger in the air. If Mom had more kids . . .

"Put your finger down!"

"How—"

"I know you too well."

"Isn't there someone?" she asked, still pleading for grandkids.

"No!" I thought about Ryan and Keira laughing about old times in the front of the Jeep. His overpowering Axe body spray still clung to my shirt. "Definitely not."

Chapter 11

Without fail, the missionaries arrived at my RV at five thirty Monday morning.

"Hi, Phil," Elder Thompson, the redhead, greeted me when I opened the door. He wore red basketball shorts and a gray t-shirt with the Arizona flag on it. Even in exercise clothes he had clipped his name badge to his shirt.

"Morning," Elder Baldini said. He looked similar, but with a white t-shirt and black shorts.

They got to work unstrapping three bicycles that were hung from a bike carrier attached to the trunk of their silver sedan. Baldini rolled a black bike with white and silver shocks on the front fork. The word "Liahona" was etched in gold stenciling.

"What's Liahona?" I asked. I wasn't familiar with the biking industry, but was certain I'd never heard of that brand before. Thompson was on a Specialized and Baldini rode on a Cannondale, both of which I recognized.

"That's a cool story." Thompson tossed me a goofy-looking helmet after he'd strapped on his own. I rolled the helmet in my hands, looking at just a stiff foam shell with a chinstrap. I didn't think I would go fast enough to test its strength, but I still didn't feel confident putting it on my skull.

We hopped on the bikes and pedaled down the gravel road. Once we hit the pavement, I stopped. "Boys, this seat is killing me and my knees already hurt."

"Hang on." Baldini put down his bike. "Bikes are our lives." He pulled out something that looked like a Swiss Army Knife. It had a bunch of Allen wrenches instead of blades. He twisted and yanked and pounded on the seat and the post. "How's that?" he asked.

I jumped on and pedaled a few feet. "I think that did it," I called. They caught up to me and we pedaled up Pinedale Road, where we turned away from town to start uphill. Thompson rode beside me, helping me figure out when to shift and which gears to use. In a few minutes we were all sucking in air as our bikes inched up the hills into a part of the area I had never seen. I thought I'd be okay, with all the running and sprinting I'd done with Keira, but the bike demanded an effort that my legs weren't used to. We climbed the hills, finding that big green cedar bushes began crowding the sides of the road.

"So, what brought you to town?" Thompson asked when the road leveled a little and we caught our breaths.

"Just drifting through more than anything," I told them.

"What do you do?" Baldini asked.

"I'm a product reviewer," I told them, trying to make it sound official.

"So you can work anywhere and just roll across the country?" Thompson asked.

"You could say that," I told him. We rode side by side by side, taking up a lane. Both of them were on either side of me.

"That's so cool," Thompson replied.

"Eh, it's okay," I told them. "So, what's this whole Liahona thing?" I asked, looking down at the word on the bike frame.

"You've been to church twice now, right?" Baldini asked.

"Yeah," I told him. Though the first time, all I could think about was food. The second time I'd spent kindling a dislike for Brozo the Clown.

"Have you seen those books that everyone carries around?" Baldini asked.

"Yeah, even the men walk around with those purse-looking book bags," I told them and they laughed.

"Well, in what you could call our main book of scripture, The Book of Mormon, there's this family that wanders around and one morning they wake up and find this ball outside their tent," Baldini explained. "They call it the Liahona. It points them in the direction they need to go."

"Like a compass?" I asked.

"Sort of," Thompson said. "Except a compass always just points to magnetic north. The Liahona pointed in the direction they needed."

"Oh, okay."

The road went uphill again and we lost our breath mashing the pedals down.

"That's it!" Thompson gasped. "I'm done."

"I win!" Baldini shouted. Thompson and I followed when he turned to coast downhill. The wind rushed over me as the treads on the tire buzzed down the asphalt. In much less time than it took to get up the hill, we were back at the RV. After we put down our bikes, the three of us sat against the RV with water bottles Baldini pulled from the car. We sat in silence, watching the sunrise turn the grass gold.

"This part of the mission makes me miss home sometimes," Baldini said.

"Where's home?" I asked him.

"San Clemente, California. You drive about ten minutes from home and it looks kind of like this. Just add the smell of the ocean and a few seagulls, and you could trick me into thinking I'm a kid again and I could ride home."

"I've been through there," I told him. "What about you, Thompson? Where's home?"

"I'm from Orem, Utah. Nothing like here."

"Never been," I said, scratching my face. "In fact, I don't even know where that is. Why didn't you get to go some place cool, like Taiwan?" I thought of Keira surrounded by Chinese people.

"Taylor's cool!" Thompson protested. We all shot glances at each other and began to laugh.

"You're thinking of Sister Brimhall, aren't you?" Baldini asked when he finished laughing.

"I mean—" I felt my face go hot "—she told me that's where she went." The two missionaries watched me with smirks.

"Right. Anyway, we're called by a prophet," Thompson said.

"A prophet?" My forehead wrinkled in suspicion. "Like a guy who talks to God?"

"Yes, exactly," said Baldini with sparkling eyes.

"Get out," I joked. "Can you prove it?"

"Yes," said Thompson, and now his eyes shone. "I wouldn't be here if I couldn't." He got up and walked over to his car. When he came back he held a small blue book in his hand. "This is why I'm here. I know this book is true, and it's kind of simple for you to know if you want to." He handed me the book.

"Well, we need to go," Baldini said as he stood up. "Can we come riding again on Wednesday?"

Keira's turquoise and cream Mini Coop pulled up. "You're going to have to ask the coach," I said, pointing to her as she got out of the car.

"Morning, Sister Brimhall," Thompson said. "Can Phil come and play with us again on Wednesday morning?"

She pulled out a notebook and looked at it. "It depends," she said, tapping a pen on her lips. "How many miles did you do today?"

"I don't know," Baldini shrugged.

I stuck my finger in the air. I thought about the time we were out and estimated the speed. "Probably only four or five miles," I said.

"If you can do eight miles on Wednesday, then you have my permission," she said.

"Thanks, Mom," I joked, making the missionaries laugh. They went to get in their car and I called out, "What about the bike?"

"You need to practice, plus no one wants it," Thompson said when got in the car. They let out a honk and drove off.

"What's that?" Keira said, smiling at the book in my hand.

I opened the door, tossing it on the couch. "Nothing?"

"It's a pretty good book," she said with a smile. "What's your breakfast going to be this morning?"

"Sis, it's going to be great. I have doughnuts, bacon, and a bagel with fresh-made strawberry cream cheese."

"Ha ha." She didn't even try smiling.

"Two egg whites and some steamed broccoli, with a treat of half a banana." My shoulders fell, depressed saying it out loud.

"All right, let's go cook," she said, opening the RV door and ushering me in.

"So, when's my first workout with Ryan?" I watched her sit on the couch with the book.

"He's going to meet us at the park this afternoon. Do you have a pen?"

"There's a pen in your hand."

"I'd like a different color."

"Over on the consul." I pointed to the front. "What am I going to have to do with Mr. Twelfth Place?"

"I know he seems like a lunk. But twelfth at the Cross Fit games really does mean something. You can't be an idiot *and* do well at that competition." She held the pen in her mouth while she flipped through the pages. Occasionally she'd stop at a page to circle something. "So he can't do things like balance a checkbook, renew the tags on his car, wash the dishes, or care for the feelings of others."

"Go on," I said, separating the white and the yolk over a small pan.

"*But*," she went on, "he can put together a program. After we divorced, I moved out here to get my master's degree online. He moved to Sedona to start his own Cross Fit box. Besides the locals that attend the box, he takes people in that Jeep to go do off-road workouts. There's a small trailer he pulls with all the equipment they need. When they get to one of those spiritual vortex things, they get out and do the workout of the day. He got the right business partner, who keeps him organized. He's doing really well."

"Couldn't he have just e-mailed my plan to you?"

"Well—" she blushed. "When I asked him I kind of hoped he would. I was a little surprised to see him at church."

"Riiiiight." I dragged it out.

"Really." She frowned.

"That's not what it looked like." I turned to her, batting my eyes. "Oh, Ryan," I said in a high voice. "Please tell me for the hundredth time about what place you got at the games. I don't want you here, but I don't mind having your arm around me the entire meeting."

"Well, have you seen the guy?" she said, looking away with a smile. "And he's sweet when he tries. When Aiko was born, you should have seen the way he was with her. Always volunteering to feed her and hold her. Aiko melted in his arms. He does care about people. Each of his clients becomes the most important person in the world. I mean, he did just drive a hundred and fifty miles to come help you."

"I bet his business partner loves that," I said, taking the broccoli bag out of the microwave. "Are you sure he's here for me?"

"He's just going to get us through the week, and then he's leaving." Her eyes pleaded with me to believe her.

"Fine," I said, carrying my plate to the table. "What are you doing?"

"I'm marking things for you to read."

"I can't just read it like a book?" I mumbled.

"Sort of," she said, circling something.

"Anyway, I already know the plot." I smirked.

She stopped and looked up. "Really?" Her eyebrows challenged me.

"Yeah, some family wanders around with a compass-like thing." I curled my lip. "It's called a Liahona."

"And?" she asked.

"Um, the ball thing points them where they should go?"

"And?" She smiled.

"There's more?"

"A lot more," she laughed.

"Fine," I said, sliding some bland egg whites into my mouth.

"Well, everything looks like it's in order here. Meet Ryan and me at three at the park this afternoon."

"You're not coming back for lunch?"

"No lunch."

"So, what are you up to today?" I asked before she got up.

"Maybe just a talk with Ryan," she said. Her hand twitched.

"About?"

"Why do you want to know?" she asked.

"Mixing this kind of business and *that* kind of a relationship is bad news. You think he was bad before?" I tilted my head, trying to look at her like a mom attempting to guilt a teenager. "You mix in a hustle, everything blows up from there," I warned.

"So you have experience with this?" She crossed her arms, clenching her jaw as she looked at me.

"Yep. You're not the only one with an ex." I decided to open up. "You ever hear of a wife carry race?"

"No." Her eyebrows popped up, prodding me for more.

"There's this race where a man has a woman over his shoulders and races other couples. It's like a mud race, but carrying a person. She goes upside down on his back and puts her legs around his head, and her arms come through his and grab her knees." I tried my best to imitate how the man carries the wife.

"Well, I found myself in Reno a couple of years back. They were going to have a wife carry race with a two-thousand-dollar prize. You see, the local marriage counselors banded together. They put the race on as a 'pay your debt' promotion. Problem is, I needed a wife. Only married couples could compete. They actually demanded certificates. Well, I was in Nevada and could get an easy marriage. I just needed a woman."

"You got married . . . just to run a race?" she asked, covering her mouth.

"Not for the race, for the prize. But hang on, I'm getting to that. So a friend told me of a friend. She drove out and met me in Reno. She really needed some money, and I really needed money and a wife." I shrugged like normal people would do something like that.

"Oh my gosh!" Her hand fell from her mouth. "You didn't!"

"Yeah, I did. But she was actually amazing. We just *got* each other. We both understood the gypsy life. Every morning and night we trained, running all around town with her on my back." I got up to put my dishes in the sink then sat next to her on the couch. "So the fake marriage actually turned into something. We won the race, and instead of splitting the money . . . we opened a joint checking account. When we left the bank, Mrs. Jenna Rae Carroll and I hopped in my van and drifted."

"Really? I guess that's romantic," she said with a forced smile.

"It was . . . for about a month. We definitely liked each other. In the end, I guess we were too used to being loners. She'd want to go one direction on a whim. If I couldn't quite calculate the need, I'd choose a different direction. She was over-spontaneous and stubborn. I got sick of the tantrums she'd throw when she didn't get her way. The coffee maker she threw at my head just about sealed the annulment. Not to mention the bookie from California who hunted her down. She was kind of a cliché con man. But a girl.

"So I turned the van around, returned to Reno, dropped her off, and annulled the marriage. I didn't look back, but I have tried to remember the lesson I learned," I said, kicking my feet up on the consul. "Lost a couple grand on the deal, too. I guess we did have some good times, though. It hurt for about a week, until I decided to clear out emotion from this kind of life. You have to be hard, calculating, and heartless." She looked at me with a frown. "To an extent." The only reason I was still in town was to help her. Had she not looked at me the way she had in the gym, I would have been long gone. Maybe I hadn't learned my lesson.

"You just left her in Reno?"

"Her car was still in the Wal-Mart parking lot where we'd left it. She threw a Slurpee I had just bought her at my van. I don't blame her. Just before I slid the door closed and locked it, I threw her keys about fifteen yards away into some bushes."

"Cold." She sat back, taking it in, her forehead creasing.

"If you'd ever met her, you'd get it. She was like a really nice wine. A really smooth drink, but before you know it, you're face down in a gutter somewhere with a Sharpie mustache on your lip." Keira gave me a fake smile, shaking her head, reminding me that she couldn't relate. "Anyway, man, she was competitive too. I carried

110

her on my back, so I couldn't see, but I'm pretty sure she hit and tripped some couples during that race."

"So what's the moral of the story?" she asked, looking out the window.

"Well, to be honest . . ." I didn't know just how to say it to her. But we did have an honesty pact. So I looked up at the ceiling to make it easier. "You are the most beautiful woman I have ever met." I knew what I'd blurted, so I continued staring at the ceiling. "You're smart, funny, interesting, and I see why Ryan would drive two hours to get here. I mean really? Samurai movies? You make it hard. Sometimes I catch myself thinking that nothing would make me happier than . . . well, let's just leave it at that."

Her head whipped around. "Excuse me?"

"That day at the break-the-fast thing, I really only agreed to working out because I thought we could go out a few times." She punched me in the arm. I cleared my throat. "But it's business now. Adding emotions to all this could ruin everything. Instead of any benefit, we could walk away broker than when we started. So what you need to understand is, if you get emotional with Ryan, we've lost."

"I can't believe you," she said, picking up a couch pillow to hit me.

"Hey, honesty pact," I shouted. I defended myself by putting my hands over my head. Instead of throwing it, she dropped the pillow and stood up.

"I'm busy during lunch. Don't eat anything dumb, and meet us at the park at three," she said, storming out.

"Aren't you going to come get me?" I asked.

"You just got a new bike. You'll burn more calories," she said before the door slammed. I watched her walk right over to Lizzie's house.

"But which park?" I whispered, watching her storm into the house.

***

Later that day when I tried making a salad for lunch, I realized I had nothing to put in it. A bowl of kale looked up at me, but I didn't have tuna, chicken, or any dressing. I nearly vomited thinking of eating straight kale. So a minute later, I knocked on Lizzie's door.

She opened the door and I held out a dollar and said, "Can I have some tuna? And maybe some salad dressing?"

Lizzie rolled her light blue eyes and told me to follow her. We passed two baskets filled with clothes in the living room. In the kitchen, Aiko sat on a stool at the counter, shoving mac and cheese into her mouth.

"Oh, that looks good," I said to Aiko, who smiled with yellow teeth. "And not so much now."

"Mouth closed," Lizzie commanded. "I do have some tuna, but just ranch dressing."

"Ehh, I guess just the tuna," I said, sitting next to Aiko and staring at her food. "Your sister would kill me if she found ranch stains on my shirt."

Lizzie walked into her pantry and said, "Speaking of my sister."

"Yes?"

She reappeared. "Beautiful? Smart? Funny? Oooh, Phil and Keira sitting in a tree, K-I-S-S-I-N-G."

We heard the door close. Lee walked in and kissed Lizzie. "I'm here for lunch. Who's kissing?"

"Keira and Phil!" Lizzie pointed to me to tattle.

Lee lifted his hands in the air. "Dude, we talked about this!"

"And dude, I heard you," I said, spinning the can of tuna on the counter, not looking at him. "Not that you helped," I mumbled out of the side of my mouth.

"What's that supposed to mean?"

"Getting her hooked on samurai flicks? Come on!" I demanded. Lee shrugged with a blank stare.

"In his defense, he drew a line," Lizzie said, stepping between us.

"See?" I pointed to Lizzie.

"Right after he called her beautiful, smart, and funny!" she added with excitement.

"And interesting," I said. Lee threw his hands in the air again.

"Nobody's ever called her interesting before," Lizzie said. "She kind of liked that. But you didn't hear that from me."

"But I explained to her what happened with my own ex-wife from Reno."

"Ex-wife?" they said together.

So I told them the story I had told Keira that morning.

Lizzie blew air out of the side of her mouth when I finished. "Wow." She now sat next to me on a stool, her chin resting on her fist.

"When did you get rid of the van? I wouldn't have to drive you around so much," Lee said. He stood next to her, eating mac and cheese.

Lizzie hit him. "That's not the point." She pulled out her phone and dialed a number.

"Keira, can I make Phil a tuna sandwich?" I heard Keira's voice on the other line. "Okay, half a can, a slice of tomato, wheat bread, and no mayo. Deal. Thanks." She hung up and put the phone back on the counter and began making sandwiches. When she finished, she slid plates to Lee and me.

Lee gobbled down his sandwich then got up and kissed Lizzie. "Don't go all Reno on Keira," he said to me as he walked out.

I got up and followed, but Lizzie ordered me to sit back down. "Phil, you're a good man."

"Eh." I shrugged. "More people than just my ex-wife that would disagree with that. Not to mention, all I do is roll from town to town finding ways to win people's money."

"No, you gave up everything for Lee and me. And Flip is too stubborn to see what you did for him. Yeah, it was dishonest to throw the match. You did it for Lee and for Flip, though. I can see past the sly weasel mask you wear. You pretend to be a calculating robot. But I know you only stayed to help Keira. So that's something. That jerk Ryan only ever treated her like she was in the way, until he needed a pretty face at his side. The first time I met you, that day you threw the match, you showed more character in five minutes than I've ever seen from stupid Ryan."

"Sis, what are you getting at?" I asked, laying my forehead on the counter.

"This isn't Reno, and Keira isn't like your ex from Reno."

"I don't know," I said into the granite. "She's looking to hustle people to help pay off her debt, so."

"Uh, well, things are just different, okay?"

My head shot up. "The last thing I want to do is leave Keira screaming at me in a Wal-Mart parking lot." We both sat in an irritating silence. I looked down at the floor, thinking about leaving my ex. "I can't blur those lines again. I'm so close . . ." I shut up and kept it to myself. I thought of my postcard from Japan. It wasn't anyone's business anymore but mine.

"Close to what?"

"Nothing. I just have to do it my way or we all lose," I grunted, standing to leave. What didn't she understand about Reno? I'd learned my lesson. "Thanks for the sandwich. I love you and Lee, and this will be over soon."

"Hold it." She turned, and I heard her searching for something in a drawer. "Turn around."

"Are you going to stab me?" I asked. But I saw she held a tape measure. "What are you doing?"

"Just turn around," she ordered, and I obeyed. "I need to see if this weight loss thing you're killing yourself over is even working." I felt the tape go across my shoulders.

"Just the belly," I told her. "That's all they're measuring."

"Oh," she said, wrapping it around my belly and then around my hips.

"Your belly is at thirty-eight."

"Great. It was forty at the weigh-in."

"Good. And now it's Aiko's nap time."

"Okay. Thanks for lunch, really, and I'm sorry," I said, walking out.

"You will be," I heard her say as the door closed.

Chapter 12

That afternoon I attempted my first ever Cross Fit workout. Even though Keira had told me to ride my bike, she and Ryan picked me up in his Jeep. He drove, top down and shirt off, to a school playground for my torture. His shaggy hair whipped in the wind. Keira sat looking down the street in the passenger seat while I endured the overwhelming blast of Axe body spray fuming off of Ryan. Ryan let out a shrill "Whoo, Cross Fit!" as he jumped out of the Jeep after parking.

After a warm-up jog around the field and a stretch session in the sand, we set to work. I had to start with a set of dips on the handles next to a slide. When I finished I ran down to the steps leading to the slide. I shoved my feet under the bottom step, where I began full sit-ups. Keira counted down from fifty. Last, I had to run the length of the soccer field and back. Then I had to do it all over again. I was supposed to do it as many times as possible in fifteen minutes. Ryan started the workout with me, but halfway through my dips he had already finished his sit-ups.

Ryan looked at his watch and finally called time during a set of sit-ups. I jumped up, ran to the edge of the sand, scooped out a hole, and began to vomit. It was mostly just the water I thought I'd drink before the workout. Hunched over the sand, lurching became its own workout. Every abdominal muscle constricted to purge my stomach. To finish, I pushed a pile of sand over the hole. Ryan cheered for me in the background with a shrill whoop.

I stumbled back to Ryan and Keira sitting on the steps of the playground. When I reached them I collapsed into the sand.

"Brotein shake, that was awesome. I really saw you leave your heart on the field. Too bad we don't have a proper box, right?"

"I'm just going to lie here in the sand for a while." My words slurred in exhaustion.

"That's how you know it worked, bro!"

I wanted to reach up and slap his perfect smile, but settled for rolling into the shade of the slide. For a few minutes, Ryan talked to Keira about Aiko.

"Do you think he can hear us?" he finally whispered. I took a deep breath to try to make it look like I was asleep. My eyes were closed, so I tried not to squish them together to appear like I was faking a nap. But I also didn't want them closed so lightly that they might flutter open.

"I don't know, why?"

"I wanted to tell you this at lunch—I still wish I knew why you canceled. You know why I really came here, right?" he asked.

"No."

"Come on, K. My life isn't right without you. How many times do I have to tell you that?"

"How many times do I have to remind you that it's over?"

"Then why did you contact me?"

"I just needed some workouts from you."

"You could have gone anywhere, K. The main Cross Fit website will give you workouts of the day."

"I didn't mean for you to think you had to come out here. Look, uh, mixing this kind of business and that kind of a relationship is bad news."

I let a smile curl the far side of my mouth when I realized she was saying exactly what I'd told her earlier. I hoped they couldn't see it.

"But I still love you. I'll always love you, sweet K."

"You can't hang on like that."

"Tell me you don't feel anything for me."

"Of course I'll always feel great . . . about the beginning."

My small smile faded.

She continued. "But the direction we were heading was destructive. I was your trophy. I did everything I thought you wanted me to do so that I could, I don't know, be worthy to be at your side. But asking anything from you to fulfill my needs was like asking you to go to prison for me. I didn't feel loved when you had me. So don't try making me feel loved now that I'm not yours anymore."

"I'm sorry," he mumbled.

"Look, just know, this is business. I'm not reaching out to be together again."

"Hmm. Well, don't be surprised when I bring my A-game. I'm fighting to get you back."

I barely heard Keira let out a long breath.

"I love you, K, and I'm sorry I didn't make you feel loved. But you can't ask me not to try. Not now that every morning I wake up thinking about how terrible I have felt without you."

I heard the step creak when he stood up. "I'm going for a jog." His feet padded through the sand and I opened my eyes again.

Keira leaned against the post that supported the slide. "You heard all that?" she whimpered.

"Yeah, sorry." I really hadn't meant to listen in. But how could I not have?

"Can you believe that? He's only here because *he* feels bad I'm not around?"

"Maybe that's not what he meant?" I rolled over on all fours and crawled to sit next to her. I didn't know what to do, so I watched the lunk jog across the field. I wanted to put my arm around her, or help her up, or say something that would make her smile again. Though she had turned to the life of a con artist, she was far from con-man material. However she had taken what Ryan had said, it was eating at her. She clenched her fists until they were white.

"It's just business, it's just business, it's just business."

"That a girl," I said, nudging her with my elbow.

Her eyes shot to me, looking me up and down. My heart raced watching her look at me. Then her shoulders dropped. "You're covered in sand. You should go brush yourself off."

Just then Ryan finished sprinting what I could only jog. "You're back up, Brobal Warming! How you feelin'?"

"Peachy," I mumbled without emotion.

"Great, let's go find a place to eat and go over the rest of the week!"

Chapter 13

The next two weeks were torture, and no, he didn't leave after a week like Keira promised. Every day I heard bro this and bro that. If Ryan had a successful business in Sedona, he sure didn't act like it. But Keira was right: Ryan developed brutal workouts. I guess that meant they were effective. Though he'd first seemed like an idiot, Ryan was much smarter than I'd originally thought. The man's brain functioned like a muscular and skeletal encyclopedia. I'd seen Cross Fitters who were idiots. Ryan wasn't one them. He meticulously planned my workouts. Ryan filled my days with burpees, sprints, push-ups, and kipped pull-ups. The fat teenager, Jeremy, and his friends were always around just in time to film me throwing up. Ryan was always there. We never had a workout without him. The three of us were like one happy family with Mom, Dad, and me—the little boy who always threw up. And of course there were some teenagers making fun of me when I did.

The only highlights of each week were the bike rides I'd go on with the missionaries. Neither of them would call me bro, tell me about burpees, or talk to me about my lumbar curve. I preferred listening to them talk about something called the "Plan of Salvation." It was much better than listening to a lecture on shoulder impingement.

Keira worked out with me to get ready for the obstacle race. She always looked composed and in her element. Some afternoons we'd all go out to the park and make a mock course. Ryan would cheer her on while trying to coach me on the correct form of whatever he felt I was doing wrong. One morning I moved my postcard from my closet door to just above the light switch next to the main door. Every time I left the Bago, I tapped the image of a Japanese temple with Mount Fuji in the background.

Lizzie always seemed mad at me when she'd see me. I got mad at me, too. There were times when I just wanted to punch Ryan's perfect teeth, spear him to the ground, and lock him in a choke. Then I could lift Keira off her feet, sell the Bago, and buy a house with a white picket fence. But I couldn't blur that line again. Adding a complexity like a woman would throw everything out of order again. It just didn't make sense to my plan. I guess things like that never do, though, and Lizzie just wouldn't give up. Her scowls were constantly reminding me that I was letting her down. So I continued tapping that postcard over and over.

One day, almost two weeks later, I finally convinced Keira to let me out of one of Ryan's torture sessions. I could do six days a week of two-a-day exercises. But Ryan being a part of my daily routine had become too much. I made up something about muscle memory, stringing together terms and theories that I had heard on numerous late-night fitness infomercials. Something I said must have been okay, because Ryan granted his approval. What I really needed was to grapple with someone and take out my frustration, and it was worth breaking the honesty pact for.

I showed up at Lee's gym and stayed for two classes, where Lee spent thirty minutes instructing and then opened the mats for sparring for the next thirty minutes. I tore through Lee's class during those open mat times. It felt good to roll, choke, arm-bar, and pounce everyone. After the last class, while Lee cleaned up the gym, I was putting on some dry clothes in the closet when he called out to me.

"That was a little too intense tonight, bud."

"Sorry," I called out. "Ryan has me pretty riled up."

"I get it. I dislocated some dude's shoulder during their divorce. That guy is bad for my students." We both laughed, but he continued when I got out of the closet. "Go help Uncle Tim clean up. That's your penance for trying to kill everyone tonight."

"All right, all right, point taken." I crossed the gym to push through the door and enter the empty Sushi Stop. More Norteño music blared from the kitchen. Tim looked up, smiling at me while he covered various tubs of food in plastic wrap.

"Lee texted me that you would help. Go ahead and trim the branches of the bonsai, then put the chairs up. The floor buffer will be here in the morning, and he gets testy when there are chairs all over the place." He reached over the bar with the scissors. "So you went a little crazy tonight?"

"Yeah, I guess so . . . *oji*?"

Tim stopped what he was doing. He looked at me, confused. "What?"

"So, I'm going to Japan. I ordered an English to Japanese dictionary that came in today."

"Why do you want to go to Japan?" he asked, still twisting his eyebrows in confusion.

I started telling him about my goal, but that spilled into telling him about my dad, dropping out of college, my nomad life, Reno, fighting my feelings for Keira, and my frustration with being around Ryan. When I finished he was still giving me an odd look. He pulled a long piece of plastic wrap to cover a tub of salmon. I had started placing the seats on the tables. The music from the kitchen ended, and one of the Mexicans poked his head through the door.

"*Adios jefe, cerraremos la puerta de atrás*," he called.

"*Gracias, Miguel. Nos vemos mañana*," Uncle Tim called back. "So what does *oji* mean?" Uncle Tim slid the last of the food in the small fridge under the bar, and then joined me in putting chairs up.

"It means uncle in Japanese."

"Why would you call me uncle in Japanese?"

"I mean, you know, you're Japanese . . . and an uncle."

"But I'm not your uncle."

"Right, but…" What was with this guy? I needed an old Asian sensei at that moment; why couldn't he see that? "Aren't you, I guess, Asian?"

"I was born in Sacramento. Just because my great-grandparents were Japanese, how does that make me Asian?"

"Whatever." I lifted the last of the chairs on to a table. "But I wouldn't hate it if you called me *oi*."

"Well, what the heck does that mean?"

"Nephew?"

"No, I've never even been to Japan."

"Fine," I mumbled. I had hoped that I could turn to him to help me get ready to one day cross the western pond to get to the Far East. He was as far from a Mr. Miyagi as I could imagine. But I had to ask, "Why do you roll sushi and have a bonsai?"

"My retirement funds are fixed. I need the money. Two Americans with Japanese heritage rolling sushi with a bonsai just made the food seem more legitimate. It's not even that good."

I laughed, thinking of shoving eight different rolls down my food- and taste-deprived throat.

"I may roll sushi and Akiyama may be my last name, but that isn't what makes me who I am. I'm a farmer from Visalia. I never got into that heritage stuff. I accept who I am."

"Oh."

"You need to relax, brother. I'm not knocking your Japan dream, but just remember. Some people get so locked on a goal that they build up some image of the outcome that doesn't end up matching what they dreamed about. Plus, why is your only answer to things to run away?"

My shoulders fell. "I don't run away."

"You ran from your martial arts, you ran from your college, you ran from your ex-wife, you're now running from your pathetic life to Japan?"

"You don't have to say it like *that*," I muttered.

"All right, well, we're looking good here. Come on, I'll drive you back to your RV."

***

Two days later, I was walking home from one grueling afternoon W.O.D., or workout of the day. I had a ring of sweat around my collar and splatters of vomit on my shirt. Ryan and Keira had stayed at the park to continue their own practice. My new bro was willing to take me home after their workout if I could wait. The thought of riding with him made me want to throw up again. I just told him that walking would burn a few more calories. That seemed to impress my new bro-rannasaurs rex.

I just kept repeating *eight grand* with every painful step I took. The cinder shoulder of the road crunched as I walked. A sudden chorus of crunching sang behind me. I turned to see a red Ford Mustang had pulled up right behind me. It revved its engine once. A hand popped out, waving me back to it. I walked up, recognizing Reggie's car from the day he had talked to us at the park.

His passenger-side window rolled down when I walked up to it. Inside he had dark leather seats. The consul, dash, and display were lit like a 747 cockpit. He had on gold aviator glasses.

"Need a ride, buddy?" he asked.

I raised an eyebrow. "What's the catch?" I asked.

"No catch, just a ride," he laughed. When he smiled his face contorted, wrinkling his neck and closing his eyes.

"Uh . . ." I looked around. It didn't feel right. "That's a vomit spot," I said, pointing to a fleck on my shirt.

"I've had much worse in this gal," he said.

I didn't want to understand what that meant. Nor did I want to understand why he found it worth bragging about.

"Well, okay." I pulled open the door. I felt a little embarrassed that my sweaty shirt was probably going to leave a salt mark. Reggie shot the car forward, passing Pinedale Road.

"Um."

"I didn't say it would be a short ride," he laughed.

Great, I thought, the opposition had kidnapped me. Maybe Keira would miss me? Would she come find my body? Would she only care if Ryan dug me up without a shirt?

"So, tough workout today?" he asked.

"Yep, employing Cross Fit," I admitted.

"Yeah, that's a grueling practice." He looked over at me and smiled. "That's the guy from Sedona, right?"

"Yep, the guy came in—"

"Twelfth in the Cross Fit games. I saw that," he finished for me.

We zoomed along the highway right out of town. The rolling hills along the road turned rocky. We entered another valley surrounded by brown cliffs. A green highway sign told us that we were entering Shumway. There were a few homes along the road, but down closer to the cliffs sat the actual town. Reggie shot off the highway, driving into the village. It wasn't much, just scattered mansions and ranches.

We drove a mile down the road, which followed a creek. The cliffs turned to shadows as the sun began setting. Reggie finally pulled into a mansion made of red logs. A big bay window looked out on cars and trucks lining the road. When we got out I felt music thumping through the cement driveway from the inside.

"Not bad, right?" Reggie asked. "This is the life when you're the big fish in a little pond. People are always asking me for a tour. Wanna take a look, buddy?"

"Well, I'm here." I shrugged.

When I stepped onto the big wrap-around porch, the music pulsed harder through my shoes. Reggie swung open the doors to a party. Girls in tight jeans and cowboy shirts were everywhere. There were a bunch of cowboys also in tight jeans, with cowboy shirts and glittering belt buckles. I blinked away the amazement. I had stepped into a hip-hop music video, except it was with cow-folk and bluegrass instead of an urban beat. A stereo system as tall as me rattled against the wall. Everyone held red plastic cups.

At the center of it all I found Kenny Blake. He didn't indulge with the rest of the party. Kenny pumped his legs on a part treadmill, part elliptical, and part stair stepper machine. He wore brand new running shoes and mid-calf tube socks. Green mesh shorts with two white stripes down the seam looked like they were spray painted on. They only covered a quarter of his thighs. He had on a blue and red mesh Detroit Pistons jersey.

"Philip Carroll! What whaaat!" he shouted when he saw me.

"What what!" Everyone stopped what they were doing to repeat him.

I gazed over his machine. Each foot stepped on a separate treadmill that moved up and down. My mouth fell open.

"State of the art custom Bowflex TreadClimber TC-one hundred," he said between labored breaths.

"Where am I?" I asked. "Who are these people?"

Reggie snapped, and two cowgirls got off of the sofa by the machine. Blake's sweat dripped steadily onto the dark hardwood floor. Reggie motioned for me to sit.

"Phil!" Blake called over the sound of the music and spinning treads. "Or should I just call you bro? How's the Cross Fit?"

I just raised my hand in the okay sign, flashing a fake smile.

Reggie reached over to put a hand on my knee.

Why do fitness people think so much touching is okay? Sure, I grapple around with sweaty men. But we're usually trying to break each other's arms. Ryan, and now Reggie, seemed to think they had a license to grope me. At least I hadn't had an "Atta boy," but that could easily change.

"Isn't this something?" Reggie asked over the noise. "He walks on this all day after he leaves my gym. It gets kind of boring and lonely, so I throw parties for him to watch occasionally."

"It sure is something," I yelled.

"Veggie tray?" He tapped a button on the arm of his chair. The end table next to him opened up, revealing a refrigerator. He pulled out a small water bottle and tossed it to Blake. Then he reached in for a tray of food. It had carrots, broccoli, cut-up mushrooms, and artichoke hearts. The vegetables surrounded an Italian dressing cup. I took a mushroom. The flavor exploded in my mouth.

"Is this a truffle?" I yelled.

"It sure is, buddy!" Reggie smiled wide.

I smiled back. "What do you want?"

Reggie whistled. The music turned down. He jumped up. "Let's make this a pool party!" Everyone cheered as they ran out the back, leaving Reggie and me in the seats. Only Blake remained, the sound of him thumping along on the treadmill echoing in the huge room.

"You want me to quit beating around the bush?" Reggie asked. I only nodded. He slapped my knee again then leaned back, throwing his arm up behind me. "A man of business. I like that!" He finally started really speaking. "You see, son. I don't want you or Keira in this town anymore." I opened my mouth to speak, but he cut me off. "Nah-uh," he said, pointing an open hand at me then snapping it shut. "Let me finish. Here's what I'm willing to do." He pulled out a roll of hundred-dollar bills. Reggie kissed it and handed it to me. "That's two thousand dollars right there."

My eyes shot open. "I, uh, what?"

"Just leave," he whispered. "You want that? Just go!"

"But—" I almost started a protest about commitment and honor.

He held his hand up again. The other hand reached into the side of his chair. Another roll of bills came out. "Another two grand? All you need to do is to leave. Just skip town. I know you wanted eight thousand. But I know you, Phil. You, buddy, are like me. You're a calculator. I've seen you." He pointed at me with the roll of bills. "I've seen you and that funny little finger in the air, doing all that math in your head."

I felt my face flush red.

"Yeah." He tilted his head to get into my line of sight. "Yeah, you're a man who can crunch some serious numbers." He held out his hand for me to give him the money back.

I hesitated.

"Doesn't it feel good?"

I couldn't help but nod.

"I could move some funds around." Reggie looked up at the ceiling and mumbled, "Maybe hand over another thousand to get Brimhall to clear town, too?"

The room began to spin. Everything inside of me screamed to hold my hand out for the rest of it. Maybe I wouldn't have quite enough to start my own place. Four grand would definitely at least get me to Japan, and then some. The only thing keeping me from reaching out was my stomach knotting up. I thought of Keira, imagining her eyes looking at me. I felt a flutter in my chest.

"So," Kenny called. "How about it?"

"I, uh," I stammered. Without thinking about it, my finger went in the air.

"Yeah!" Reggie shouted. "That's it right there."

My hand fell.

"Tell you what, son! You take the night and do your little calculator thing." He pulled a one-hundred-dollar bill out. I watched him write a phone number on the bill. "Call me tomorrow and let me know? This here is a little consideration fee I'm paying you." He handed me the bill.

"Uh, I," I kept stammering. Four grand tempted me. It would be a huge boost to the Japan budget.

Reggie jumped to his feet. After I stood, he swatted my butt.

"There it is," I muttered.

"I like you!" he shouted and laughed.

The party returned to the living room when we left, the cowgirls and boys now only wearing their swim shorts and bikinis.

He led me back to his car. After just a few minutes of questionable driving and near-felony speeds, he dropped me off at the Bago.

Chapter 14

The sun had just about finished setting when I walked up to the Bago. Lizzie leaned against my door with a garment bag. "You look disgusting," she said with a grimace at the dried vomit stains on my shirt. "What's with the Mustang? Was that Reggie?"

I faked a smile. "Someone thought I needed a ride. What's this?" I asked.

"Don't you remember?"

"Remember what?" One of my eyebrows crept up.

"You promised to take Keira to the dance?" She put a hand on her hip, tapping a foot on the cement.

"Dance?"

"Yeah, the World War II dance?"

"I mean, I thought—" I didn't know what to say. That was the last thing I had been thinking about. I took the bag from her and unzipped it to find a green jacket with brass buttons and military patches. She smiled at me. Then it dawned on me why she had actually measured me that past week. Lizzie hadn't cared about my belly size; she had customized a coat for me.

"No," I told her. I walked past her to get to my door.

"Want to find a new driveway?" she asked.

I lifted my finger in the air and calculated the possible price of a trailer park for another month. I frowned. "No."

"Go clean up and put this on with your khaki pants," she ordered. "I've taken the liberty of shining your shoes, too. They're not exactly replica, but they'll work and they're on the couch. By the way, I've made you a captain."

"Fine," I said, defeated, snatching the bag out of her hand.

"You have forty-five minutes. She thinks I'm going with her, but I'm going to tell her that Aiko's sick." She handed me a paper with black and white pictures of World War II soldiers. "Do your hair like them."

"Okay," I said as the door shut. My shoulders slumped forward in defeat as I pulled myself into the RV. My whole body hurt from the insane workout Ryan had put me through. I was tired, hungry, and sick of him. My mind still reeled from holding four thousand dollars in my hand only to give it back. Now I had a decision to make. Do I reach out for the four grand and leave?

My freshly shined shoes and a hat sat on the couch. It looked like the kind of military hat they wore in the old movies, with the dark glossy bill. I rolled my eyes and started getting cleaned up. The weeks since starting the competition had shot by. Wasn't the dance on a Saturday? Was today Saturday? I had lost track of the calendar.

Keira arrived earlier than Lizzie had said she would. The moon reflected on her Mini Coop when I walked out of the RV. She honked right as she pulled into the driveway. I saw her head tilt in confusion. She got out, wearing a dark blue forties dress with white polka dots. Her red heels and her red beaded necklace complimented the blue dress. She'd done her shiny dark hair in victory curls with a red rose on the side.

My mouth fell open, speechless. I just wanted to retreat back to the RV. The line I'd drawn, at that moment, looked pretty blurry. It blurred more with each second I looked at her. The tips of my ears tingled thinking about dancing with her. The bad part was that I had no idea how to dance. What kind of dancing did they even do back then? I'd once tried a break dance competition that I never should have tried because the results were terrible. Especially since I hurt my ankle.

"What's going on?" she asked as she began running her hand over the dark olive green jacket. My skin tingled where she touched me. Lizzie had stitched an American flag on one shoulder. A white *A* in a blue circle with a red ring around it was stitched on the other. Two silver bars were on the shoulder loops of the jacket. I held the hat in my hand. She smiled as she took it and placed it on my head. I grimaced, knowing she might ruin the part in my hair I'd worked so hard on. Then she canted it to the side.

"Ask your stupid sister," I muttered, walking with her across the yard and up to the door. It opened before we knocked. Lizzie rushed out with Aiko screaming inside.

"Keira, I'm so sorry, Aiko came down with a fever and I'm going to stay with her. Phil is going to take you for me," Lizzie said. Keira walked past her to see Aiko. When she knew Keira couldn't see her, Lizzie smiled at me, giving me a thumbs up. When Keira looked back at us, Lizzie dropped her hand. Keira's gaze went from Lizzie to me, then back to Lizzie.

"And he just happened to have a custom-fit replica World War II uniform lying around?"

Lizzie looked at me, biting her lip.

"What can I say? Sometimes I own weird things for weird reasons," I said, staring at the ground.

Lee walked out. He took one look at me and started laughing. "Oh no, Phil, don't nuke one of my cities!" he said.

Lizzie punched him. "You can't say that!"

"*I* can," Lee laughed.

The flash of headlights on the driveway interrupted us. A matte olive green Jeep with a white star on the hood

pulled up. When it parked behind Keira's car, we saw
Ryan in the driver's seat. He hopped out and came
running to us. He wore an old field jacket with tan pants
that he'd bloused with the ankle things the GIs wore over
dark brown boots. He had a clean shave, and he'd cut his
hair short. He looked larger and more intimidating in the
uniform.

"Look what I did to the Jeep!" he cried.

Lizzie walked inside, slamming the door before I
heard her start swearing. Keira and Lee were between
Ryan and me. The two of them just looked back and forth
at us. Lee finally gave up, smiled, and wished us good
night. When he opened the door I could still hear Lizzie
swearing.

"Bro-chacho! You're coming too? Sweet, let's go,"
he said, taking Keira by the arm to the Jeep. I followed
behind, though it would have been simple enough just to
walk into the RV and go to sleep. When we were all in
the Jeep, Ryan put a netted steel helmet on his head.
"This is going to be awesome! Let's go get some Japs!"

"Okay, *you* can't say that," I said.

***

I sat in the corner of the social hall with my hat pulled
low, watching Keira and Ryan dancing. My feet were up
on a white folding chair. The big room was decorated
with flags and posters for recruiting and war bonds. A
high school jazz band was in one corner, playing forties
big band music. Everyone was dressed in period clothes.
There were soldiers, sailors, marines, airmen, nurses,
Rosie Riveters, and more. I sulked in the corner,
watching Sergeant America swing dance with Keira. She
smiled and laughed with a glow. Her lips pursed as she
would take his hands to slide under his legs. Then he'd

step over her, swinging her back to her feet. When they did that, her wide smile made me sick. I couldn't help but let out a small growl when he'd smile back.

I filled my mind with all the best wrestling takedowns I could try on Mr. Smooth Feet. He was big and his legs were thick, so I'd be better off with a double-leg takedown. But if he knew how to sprawl I'd be in trouble. All that muscle could easily fall on my shoulders. With a strong grip on the lapel, though, it seemed thick enough for a good judo-toss over my hip. That would really stun him. If we both went down, a guy like that could get on top of me. I smiled thinking about all the moves I could do on him. That's right where I'd want him.

"Reno," I whispered. That did nothing. Keira had more fun and smiled more than I had ever seen before. Maybe his charm had really worked this time. I rolled my eyes, thinking that he wouldn't even be back if I hadn't been here in the first place. Also, why did I care so much? This was just supposed to be a partnership. It was an easy one. Our rewards were clearly defined. Just then, Ryan lifted her in the air and started swinging her around his hip.

My glare hardened. I didn't want him to dance with her. *I* wanted to dance with her. I wanted to hold her, and kiss her, and walk through the fields holding her hand. That should be *me* making her smile. That's when I imagined picking Ryan up over my head. I'd summon superhuman strength to throw him into the cardboard cutout of a tank along the wall. Or, since that was unlikely, I could go over and jump face-first into the silver platter of cookies!

Someone tapped me on the shoulder, interrupting my violent fantasy. A girl in a nurse's outfit with long golden brown hair extended her hand and asked me to dance. With nothing else to do, and not wanting to be a jerk, I took her hand. The music calmed down with the clarinet slowly leading the music as we walked out on the floor. I led her to a spot on a dance floor right where I could see Keira. When did I transport into an eighties movie? I didn't really know what to do, so we just swayed from side to side as I glared at the two of them.

The nurse and I made small talk as the band played. I'll admit that I don't remember what we were saying since I was watching Keira and Ryan dancing. She had a huge smile as he twirled and dipped her. He pulled her in close and began whispering to her. My teeth tightened. The battery of my phone had gone dead playing games trying to avoid watching those two dance. I almost asked the nurse girl for her phone. I wanted to have Lee come and get me, or I could have called Reggie. His hundred-dollar-bill was still in my wallet. I paused when Keira suddenly pushed Ryan away and stormed off. Everyone stopped dancing to watch. He didn't know what to do. The blonde nurse and I just stood there. Ryan held something small in his hand, but I focused Keira.

"Sorry," I told the nurse. "I better check on my coach."

I ran after her as she pushed the doors open. She stood under a lamp with her arms tensed and her fists clenched.

"Ma'am, are you all right?" I asked, taking off my hat.

"Just, no. The idiot sold his Cross Fit box!"

"So?" I asked.

"He bought a ring and proposed again." Her hand flew to her face to smack her forehead.

"And?" I said anxiously, my heart pounding.

"I can't believe him. You should have heard him. 'Keira baby,'" she said, imitating him. "'You belong with me.'"

"Romantic," I said.

"He sold everything all because I *belong* with him?" She crossed her arms, turning to me.

"I don't know what to tell you, sis," I said, taking a step toward her.

"And there you are, watching me all night and not dancing with me once."

"I can't . . . wait, what?" My eyes widened as I tried to figure out what she'd said. Whatever it was, I thought it meant something good. I felt a smile starting.

She lifted her hand to started rubbing the bridge of her nose. "You could have burned some calories . . . or something."

"What *something* are you talking about?" I asked, taking another step toward her again.

"Nothing," she said, turning away. I rolled my eyes. This was going to be my last chance to keep things professional. I almost did it. But she called my name when I turned away to find that nurse and ask for her phone.

"You think I'm interesting?" she asked, looking up at me the hint of a smile on her lips.

"Yeah." I shrugged.

"And?" she asked.

"Gorgeous, smart, funny. I've never trusted anyone more than you." I smiled, taking another step closer. "I mean, my world hasn't made sense since I met you."

"You've been looking at me different for a couple of weeks."

I felt my face turn hot. "I can't stop wanting to carry you away to watch a samurai movie."

Even with the yellow glow of the lamp, I saw her blush. She turned her back to me under the light. I felt myself walk over to her. It surprised me when I spun her around. I took her hand in mine. Her hand squeezed mine. Then I put my other hand on her hip. "I'm not like the golden boy—I can only rock side to side," I warned her, looking deep into her eyes. She put her hand on my shoulder and we began to sway. The soft music from inside was enough for us. She let go of my hand, resting hers on my other shoulder. I put my other hand on her waist.

She looked up at me. I brought my forehead down and rested it on hers as we kept swaying back and forth. Her hand ran through my hair, brushing against my ear. My hand moved up her side, resting against the side of her head. The lamp, the moon, the streetlights all sparkled in her eyes. I pulled her face in and she lifted herself on her tippy toes. Our lips pressed against each other's. When I felt her smile and heard her sigh, I knew the line I had desperately tried to establish had just evaporated.

Chapter 15

All my supposed professionalism disappeared.

Obviously I hadn't learned my lesson when I'd made the mistake in Reno. Now I watched myself making it again. I have no recollection of how we got back to Lee and Lizzie's house, since we had arrived with Ryan. I don't remember or care what happened to him, either. That kiss made the world flip, and we could have floated home, for all I know.

We did get back somehow. Sitting on the porch steps with my back to the railing, I held Keira in my arms and she leaned back against me. I covered her in the green army jacket Lizzie had made for me. The two of us watched the stars. Her fingers pointed to the sky, tracing what I thought were the constellations. She'd bring it back down to place her hand on my cheek, making sure I was still there. I'd turn and kiss the palm of her hand so she'd know I was.

"So...?" I asked, raising an eyebrow.

"Mm-hm?"

"You wanted me to come dance with you?"

"Mm-hm."

"I'm not complaining, but . . ."

"But what?" she asked, lightly smacking my cheek.

"Why?" I asked. What about me made her want me to come steal her away from the doctor of biceps? I was a mediocre hustler who lived in a Winnebago. That's not something that projects security or maturity.

She took her time to think about it.

"Does it really take that long to think about it?"

"No . . . . And yes."

"Ah, that's helpful, and slightly painful," I mumbled.

"No, I didn't mean it like that." She reached up to grab my hand with both of hers. Her thumbs traced my knuckles.

"What you meant was?"

"You're likeable . . ."

"Gee, thanks?"

"No, I mean I don't know. A couple of weeks ago when you said those things—"

"The most beautiful woman I have ever met? You're smart, funny, and interesting?"

Her head fell back onto my shoulder. "Yeah, those things," she sighed. "I guess that kind of opened my eyes. Watching you watch us infuriated me. *You* make me laugh and have fun. It should have been you on that dance floor with me. Since Ryan has been here, you've been aloof and hadn't made me laugh. I missed that about you."

"Well. He *is* a better dancer." I shrugged. Her hand clamped down on the soft spot on my knee.

"Anyway," she continued after she was satisfied she'd inflicted enough pain and grabbed my hand again. "I feel like you look at me for more than anything Ryan ever saw. I always felt like just a trophy to him. He'd only pull me off the shelf when he needed someone on his arm to make him look good. When we were alone he always coached me on what to do better. I couldn't take it anymore. You don't do that. You listen to me. I mean, you chided me for my school debt. But even then, you weren't actually trying to polish me—"

"I mostly laughed at your situation," I confirmed.

Her hand clamped down on my other knee, squeezing it and making me yelp. "Right," she said. "You still didn't do it because you're better than me and stooping to my level to pour out your grace upon me."

"Yeah that's one way to put it."

"So," she said, still caressing my hand. "You broke your rule. You crossed the line."

I thought about more than that. I could feel the weight of Reggie's money roll in my palm.

"Well, there may be good news. An escape pod just opened up." My forehead wrinkled.

She turned to look at me. The stars and Lee's porch light shimmered in her eyes. "What does that mean?"

I told her about my ride with Reggie and the visit to Kenny's party. When I finished, she bit her lower lip.

"So what are you going to do?" she whispered. I felt her hand begin to shake.

"Watching you dance with him almost pushed me to call him. I was going to call Lee to come get me. Then I would have dialed the number Reggie gave me. I want the eight grand, but four could still put me where I want to be. Even twenty-five hundred could—"

"What do you mean, twenty-five hundred?"

"Well, he offered another grand to get you to quit." She spun around to look at me. Before she could interrupt, I continued. "We could split the five. You need the money. I need the money. Shoot, I'd take you to Japan with me. I mean, if you wanted to, or whatever."

"But—"

"I'm just saying we have an out."

"Is that what you want?"

"I want eight grand. Being here, with grounded people like Lee and Lizzie, has been really tempting me to finally put some roots down. Now with you here in my arms, I want my own gym . . . I want you. And that means I want Japan. But I saw Kenny's set-up. Reggie has him churning calories. This guy knows his stuff. His offer gave us a large bird in the hand, sis."

"First"—one of her eyebrows shot up—"now that we're on a kissing basis. Don't call me sis anymore."

"That is a valid concern." I rested my chin on her shoulder, waiting for her answer to the competition.

"I want to go for it." She placed her palm on my cheek. "Yes, we could take the money. But like I said earlier, *this* is home. I want to be close to my niece and my sister. I want to be close to my parents," she choked. She took a deep breath. "I think we can do this. He's in his forties and I'm still in my twenties. Sort of. I'm still counting twenty-nine as my twenties. Kenny may think he's on top of the food chain, but you and me? We can do this." She turned around to throw her lips into mine. When she pulled away, looking deep in my eyes, she whispered, "Phil, we got this."

My head floated from how hard she kissed me.

"Oh, crap." She jumped up.

"What?"

"The sun's coming up. I have to get ready for church." I looked at the fading stars and the sky transforming from deep blue to dark purple.

"Can't we skip this week?" I said, willing the sun to stay where it was.

"No," she said, handing me the coat. "We're going." She stood up, leaned over, and kissed me, lingering for a moment. I watched her walk over to her car. When she was in and had turned on the car, she blew me a kiss before driving off.

I sat watching the sun light up the clouds. A few minutes later, the door behind me opened and softly closed. Lizzie, in a robe, a white t-shirt, and sweats walked across the porch, dragging her slippers. She looked down at me with squinted eyes, rubbing them with the sleeve of her robe. Her hair was a mess.

"That bad, huh?" she asked. "Did you sleep on my porch?"

"No. And no." I forced a fake frown.

Lizzie sat down next to me on the steps.

"So what happened last night?" she asked.

"Ryan proposed to Keira," I grunted as I stretched.

She swore. "I'm sorry I sent you." She leaned her head on my shoulder. "Wait." She put her nose on my sleeve. "Why do I smell Keira's perfume?"

I just looked at the clouds and watched the still-rising sun turn them pink.

"Why?" She poked me in the rib.

"Lizzie, your sister's lips are soft."

She gasped, jumped to her feet, and began pacing back and forth on the porch. "I can't believe it. It worked. I mean it was my plan, so of course it worked. What happened to Ryan? How did you get home?" She stopped dead in her tracks. "What have you two been doing all night?"

"Just sitting here talking," I said, sticking my hands in the air.

"Aww," she sighed and fell into one of the rocking chairs. "I get the credit."

"You get the blame if it all explodes," I said. I began anticipating a violent emotional crash like the last week with my ex-wife. We constantly yelled and she threw various hotel objects at me. I couldn't help but remember her pounding on the sliding door when I left her in the Wal-Mart parking lot, and then the Slurpee exploding on the window. Luckily I beat her to the Justice of the Peace and ended our marriage before she could protest. It helped that I'd thrown the keys to her car into the bushes twenty yards away.

"Give me your pants," I heard Lizzie say.

"What?" I whipped around.

"I need to wash them before church."

"Oh." I relaxed. "Do you like your life?"

"What?"

"Do you do what you want?" I asked her. Weeks before at dinner, Keira had made it sound like Lizzie was what Keira was supposed to be. It had bugged me thinking about it. With King Pecs dictating my life, and Lizzie mad at me most of the time, I'd never found a good time to ask her.

"Of course."

"But, you run around picking up after Aiko and Lee?"

"And you," she added with a frown.

"Right, and you cook for us, wash our clothes. Do you do it because you're supposed to?"

"Yes, the list goes on and on and repeats itself over and over." She looked at the light creeping across the hills. "There's nothing you're *supposed* to be."

"It just seems like all you Mormon moms are supposed to be at home while you send your husbands out to work."

"By that thinking, I'm supposed to be married in the temple, too."

"Yeah, I don't really know what that means . . ."

"Back when this town was just a farming settlement, I guess there were roles that everyone expected from each other. Wives did have to run the home. Husbands had to go out into the fields, hunt, build. Someone had to be a blacksmith, a teacher, and a few other professions. Now? There aren't any expectations like that anymore. I believe as long as you follow the Lord's principles, whatever you do in your twenty-four hours doesn't matter. I want to be here with Aiko right now. When she goes to school, maybe I'll go do something else. Either way, no one should feel that my twenty-four hours are what theirs are supposed to be."

"Huh," I grunted. I hadn't thought about that. I waited a minute, watching the sun light the hills, then told her I'd be back with my pants.

Chapter 16

Somebody spoke at the pulpit, and then someone else did. I didn't really care what happened during sacrament meeting. I sat next to Keira against the wall holding her hand. Lizzie put herself and Aiko between Lee and us. She must have had the same fear of his reaction had he found out that I'd strictly disobeyed his wishes. Though I figured if we were serious about a relationship, he probably wasn't going to mind.

Keira and I didn't go to Sunday School. We ditched and walked around the building a few times and down the road a bit and back. We claimed that it was for me to burn calories. At least that's what we told each other. Really we just wanted to hold hands. Under the shade of a large tree on someone's property, we might have kissed a little too. But she got me back in time for the last meeting.

The priesthood meeting went on forever. I just wanted to be with Keira, but I had to wait while some guy umm-ed and uhh-ed reading out of some book. I hoped that Keira felt the same. That in her women's meeting she sat ready to run through the doors and wrap her arms around me.

We couldn't hide it anymore when we got back to Lee and Lizzie's. We hadn't slept for almost twenty-four hours. The two of us fell asleep on the couch next to Lee's recliner while Lizzie made dinner. And we weren't just napping, but fast asleep spooning right in front of him.

He flaunted his disappointment during dinner. Lee smashed his fork into the meatballs in his spaghetti while staring at me eating my salad. I tried to avoid his gaze, but when Keira rested one of her feet on mine I accidentally let out an involuntary sigh. The murderous stab of another meatball interrupted my brief ecstasy.

Lizzie made Lee do the dishes alone to let Keira and me retreat to the porch, where we sat and rocked for hours. I watched her as she planned my week for me. I watched her eyebrows move up and down, scrunching her forehead lines. I watched her lips open and close. Her eyes watched the sky and the hills while she told me what we should do that week.

Well after the sunset had painted the white clouds red, yellow, and purple and finally drifted past the horizon, we said an anxious goodbye. She kept insisting that I needed a full eight hours of sleep. I argued that *dreaming* of her wasn't enough, but she said that it would have to do. I finally let her leave with a kiss. Yeah, I became that sappy. And when she left, I pulled the hundred-dollar bill out of my pocket to call Reggie with my final answer.

"Phil? This is Phil, right?"

"Yeah, it's me."

"So? Bags are packed, right?"

I looked over the fading light on the hills. "I have a great view right where I am. I think I'm staying for awhile."

He didn't answer for a moment.

"Phillip," he strained. "Phil. I'm giving you one last shot. Tell me you're leaving."

"Nah, I'm going to take a hard pass."

"I'm going to destroy you," he growled, right before the line went dead.

***

Lee pounded on my door early that next morning.

"You're coming with me," he said. I followed him out the Winnebago without tapping the postcard. A chill bit me when I stepped outside. Lee mumbled something I couldn't hear as he stomped to his car.

"The missionaries are coming to ride with me."

"I already called them and canceled it," he said.

He drove in silence. We turned into town, which was a relief. I thought he wanted to take me into the forest past the hills and bury me there.

We pulled up at his gym and I followed him in. We both took off our shoes. As soon as he turned the lights on he speared me to the mat. He jumped on my side and I fought to push him between my legs to get to guard, but he put all his weight on my shoulder. The way his shoulder ground my face showed me how seriously he was taking this. He began rolling at full speed, and it took me a moment to ramp up to his intensity. But before I could, he grabbed my wrist, wrenched it backward, and held it there. Even when I tapped on him he waited an extra second.

He let me get to my knees and then attacked me again.

"I told you to leave Keira alone. She's basically my sister and you didn't listen," he growled.

I threw my legs up and tried to catch him in my guard again, but he was so mad that he fought faster than I had ever seen him. He had my ankle in his armpit and lay back, stressing my tendons and joints. I tapped again and he slowly released and let me get back to my knees.

"Ryan re-proposed on Saturday night at the dance," I said between heavy breaths.

Lee positioned himself to pounce on me again, but that stopped him for a moment. We both got to our feet while he contemplated, but his face glared at me again and he jumped at me. This time I was more prepared and sprawled backwards, stuffing his attack.

I wrapped an arm around his neck like a front headlock and fell to my back to try a guillotine. It was easy enough for him to counter, and soon his head popped out. He kicked his legs in the air and got past my legs, controlling my side again. He feigned an attempt to lock my shoulder back again but instead stepped one leg over mine and mounted my chest. He leaned forward, trying to crush my diaphragm with his hips.

I grabbed my elbows with my hands to push up on him to get some space. He spun around and trapped one of my arms between his legs. My other arm hung on to the trapped one with all my strength. Then he went with a dirty move. Not dirty as in cheating. He put his bare foot on my cheek to push my neck away. A leg is stronger than an arm. It broke the grip of my defense. I tapped again and he held my arm just to the point of breaking. Then he let me go. We repeated the beating for another fifteen minutes. I'd get up to my knees and he'd attack me again. I became desperate trying match his intensity. Being the more experienced grappler, he kept outwitting me and tapping me.

Finally I gave up and just lay on the mat. Sweat poured down my face and pooled on the mat. My chest heaved in and out for air.

"You're cleaning that up!" he shouted and went to fill up the bucket.

"Why are you so mad? This is all Lizzie's fault. Plus, don't you think I'm good for her?" I panted.

"It's not about you being good for her," his voice boomed from the maintenance closet. "Sure, maybe you'll be good together. But *I* asked you to back off. I was fine with you making puppy dog looks at her for weeks."

"I didn't make puppy dog looks," I mumbled as I began stretching my legs and hips.

"But you disrespected my wishes. I've seen her hurt before, and you said yourself this has the potential to be a disaster. So pardon me for being protective of my sister-in-law!" he roared.

The front door swung open, ringing the bell above it. Jeremy and his friend with the camera walked in. He looked at me and raised his eyebrows, surprised to see me.

"What are you doing here?" I asked.

"Uh, a private class?" he asked more than stated.

"Jeremy," Lee called, looking from the closet to see who it was, "Come on in."

"What's he doing here?" I asked Lee as he rolled the bucket and mop to me.

"What? He wanted to do a few private sessions," Lee said, hugging the kid.

"Yeah," Jeremy said more definitively. He fished in his pocket and handed Lee a twenty-dollar bill. "Sometimes people make fun of me," he asked more than stated.

I got up and began wiping up my sweat puddle with the mop and disinfectant. I looked at them with a raised eyebrow. Lee, Jeremy, and the camera boy watched me watch them.

The bell rang as the door opened again.

"Where is he?" I heard Ryan's voice boom.

I spun around and stared at Keira's large and beefy ex-husband. His jaw clenched and he flexed his biceps.

Veins popped out of his forehead—and every other muscle in his body.

"Are you taking privates from Lee too . . . bro?" I asked.

"You stole my wife, man!" He shouted and walked toward me. "Not cool, bro." He went to step on the mat but Lee suddenly screamed.

"Aaahhh! Shoes off!" Lee shouted.

Ryan's face turned red. "Oh yeah, sorry, Lee."

"Let the mats dry and then you can tear each other apart!" Lee shouted.

"Okay," Ryan replied with a frown. He went and sat on a folding chair by the front door. His knees bounced up and down, his calves flexing like footballs. He put his head down, watching the floor with his hands covering his ears.

When Lee had attacked me, I half figured that I deserved it. He had in fact told me to back off. Then he saw us spooning on his couch. Now that Ryan had arrived, my testosterone pumped through my veins. I paced back and forth, watching Ryan wait for the mats to dry. I thought about my strategy. Him being bigger and stronger could be a problem had I not been smarter.

Jeremy and his friend sat in the other chairs, smiling from ear to ear. They couldn't have had any idea why the room was so filled with tension. They just saw two grown men ready to tear each other apart and they couldn't wait to film it. Jeremy had his phone up and his friend had staged a GoPro.

"He's strong. Gym strong, but still," Lee whispered with a smile.

"Yeah, I heard," I said. "Twelfth place in the Hunger Games, right?"

Ryan's head shot up. "Cross Fit Games!" he yelled.

We watched with anticipation as the wet marks on the mat faded like we were waiting for high noon. Lee walked over and slid his foot across the mat to check. "All right, boys, you clean your own blood," he said allowing us on the mat.

"Rules?" Ryan asked.

"Whoever walks or crawls out that door loses," I growled, pointing at the door.

"OOOOOOHHHH, snap!" Jeremy said from behind his phone. He lowered his voice to sound like a ring announcer. "Two men enter, one man, uh . . . walks out?"

"Just do it. You're burning Jeremy's time," Lee said.

I lunged at Ryan, got my shoulder between his legs, and lifted him like a fireman. He yelped as I rolled him over, slamming him to the mat. His arms flailed out. I moved in on him and instantly controlled his side, pinning my knee to his ribs. I slid my foot over his arm, stretching one arm with my legs and trapping the other between my neck and my shoulder. I had a free hand and lightly smacked his cheek. "Come on, Mr. Twelfth Place," I said. I released his arms and rolled away. Lee had had his fun; now it was my turn.

He got to his knees and flew at me. I caught his head in a front headlock and threw my legs around his waist in the guard. I held him firmly but light enough to let him breathe. "Are you sure that's the right move to make?" I said and then pressed my hips up. My arms and hands slowly choked him and I felt him squirming. I eased up and asked, "Again?"

Lee was right: Ryan had strength. When I relaxed, he got his hands up on my elbow and chest and pushed his head out. A slight mat burn across his forehead began turning red.

"Handstand push-ups, jackass!" he yelled.

"Fine," I said, relaxed. I still had him in my guard, controlling his hips. He tried to stand but I fished under one of his ankles and pushed my legs forward, toppling him backwards. He tried to control his fall by squatting down, but I still had an ankle. I wrenched it up into my armpit and his back thudded down.

"OOOHHHH!" Jeremy cheered.

I pushed forward with my legs and leaned back, pulling his ankle. Ryan's face flushed bright red. He grimaced, showing all his teeth. Finally he started slapping at my feet. "All right! All right!" he cried. I released him and did a reverse somersault to show off. I jumped up and beat my chest. I'd wanted to do that since I'd first heard all that *twelfth place* stuff.

Ryan stood up, limped over to his shoes, and walked out the door. Jeremy and his boys were jumping around hollering.

"I'm putting that to music!" one of them shouted.

"All right, shut up!" Lee called. The teenagers died down. "Turn those off. Jeremy and I are going to train. Phil's walking home to think about his actions."

I put my shoes back on. "Fine," I said. "Mid-weigh-ins are soon anyway. I could use the walk." I walked out when half the sun had risen on the horizon. Ryan's now-green Jeep sped out of the parking lot and went north on Main Street. Grunting, I went south on foot. My knees were burning from rubbing on the mats and I even felt a stinging on my ear. Lee must have head-butted me at one point.

I hoped my ear wasn't going to swell as I got to Pinedale road. I heard a familiar wimpy honk from behind. I smiled, knowing Keira's Mini Coop had just pulled up behind me. I turned around and saw her beautiful smile then went to open the passenger side door. It was locked and wouldn't budge. She laughed and rolled the window down.

"You keep walking, mister! Is your RV unlocked?"

"It's locked, but I have the keys right here. I'll give them to you for a kiss."

"Well, come over here and I'll pay up," she said.

I giggled like a teenager and tried to slide across her hood. For some reason it wasn't as slippery as I thought. My butt stopped sliding but my upper body kept moving forward. I sprawled out on her hood for a second, then rolled off onto the gravel of the shoulder.

It hurt my pride, but nothing else. I jumped and stuck my arms up like a gymnast. Keira laughed at me and called out, "Ten!" from the window. I walked over with a fake limp.

"I think I need a rubdown?" I suggested with a whimper.

"Yeah?" she said, reaching for my keys. "How about some post-run breakfast?" she puckered her lips.

"I wasn't running, uh, I need to tell you something when I get home," I said, leaning over to kiss her. I closed my eyes and found my lips touching her hand.

"Why do you smell like Ryan?" she asked. Her lips scrunched together.

I grunted a little, upset that she could still remember what her ex-husband smelled like. "Well, that's what I need to tell you." I rubbed my hands together with a deep gulp.

"I can't wait to hear!" she said, driving off.

The thoughts that ran through my head the next mile terrified me. What was she going to think? First I hoped she would go talk to Lee and give him a piece of her mind. What gave him the right to tell her whom she could date? At least that's what I wanted her to think. I was mostly afraid of her reaction to Ryan. My feet crunched up the gravel road and I knocked on my RV.

"Come in," she said.

I walked in and stood behind her. "Hi?" I asked.

"Shower." She pointed to the bathroom.

I walked in to find she had laid clothes out for me. "You went through my stuff?" I was a little embarrassed thinking of her touching my underwear.

"Just go stink less," she ordered as she violently scrambled some egg whites.

My shoulders slumped forward. "Yes, ma'am." Was I in trouble? I didn't do anything. First, I was persecuted for our love. So that should be a plus. And then Ryan challenged me for her honor. So I thought I was justified.

I tried to clean up as fast as I could. I bumped into everything trying to get dressed in the tiny bathroom. I began to panic. The closer I got to facing her, the harder my heart pounded. When I walked out into the tiny living room, I found Keira at the table. An empty chair in front of a plate with the scrambled egg whites and some Greek yogurt waited for me.

"Sit," she ordered.

"Yes, ma'am," I mumbled, plopping on the seat.

"Speak."

"Well…" I started going over my morning. I told her every detail. I may not have mentioned how bad Lee had beaten me, but I did mention he was mean about it. I added how bravely I defended myself against him. Her brows furrowed while I spoke. It was impossible to read her face. My palms were getting sweaty. A bitter taste filled my mouth, but that might have been the plain Greek yogurt. When I finished I looked at her for approval.

"Okay." She shrugged.

"That's it?" I asked.

"Yes." She finally smiled. "What do you want me to do, jump into your arms and call you my hero?"

"Uh . . . yeah!" I declared. "I fought for you honor!" I said with another spoonful of yogurt in my mouth. "Against two foes!" I tried my best to sound chivalrous.

"I guess you could see it that way," she said.

"How do *you* chose to see it?"

"Three meat heads showing off." Her eyes rolled. "This isn't the days of cavemen. Why couldn't you just talk about it?"

"I didn't do much showing off," I laughed, thinking about my one-sided victory.

"Boys." She rolled her eyes again.

"What about Lee?" I asked, offended that she hadn't seen me as a victim yet.

"What *about* Lee?"

"He, uh . . ." I didn't know where to go. "He thinks he can tell you who to date! Yeah, that's it. You are a strong, independent woman who doesn't need a man telling her what to do."

"And yet I need one to beat up my ex?" Her eyebrows went up, challenging my story. "And I thought Lee's attacks were ferocious. Didn't you bravely fend them off?"

"Well, they *were* ferocious," I mumbled, pushing some of my egg around with a fork.

"Aww, poor baby, my big brother pushed you around a little?"

"Thank you, that's what I've been waiting for. My ear hurts a little. It might swell some." I tried to milk it as much as I could.

She got up and kissed my ear.

"I meant the other one?" I spun and offered her the other side of my face. She kissed that one too.

"Where are you going?" I asked as she reached for the door. "Don't you want to do something?"

"You seem to have had your workout for the morning," she said.

"But . . ."

"I'll see you at lunch." She blew a kiss and left.

Chapter 17

Spending most of our time together for almost two weeks passed by too quickly. The postcard reminding me about Japan became an afterthought. Just tapping it before I left felt like wasted time I could be with Keira. I figured watching Samurai movies with her every now and then would keep me focused still.

Somehow she found a bike of her own and began coming on morning rides with the missionaries and me. The rides became tag-team sessions. The three of them would take turns saying something churchy. I didn't pay much attention. I silently rode next to her since I just liked listening to her talk to me. My only drive was now to win the competition to keep her smiling.

Thursday marked the half-point weigh-in. It would give a good gauge of where we were going. Hopefully it would also break a few spirits and some people would drop out. We were back at the high school gym, staring at the big scale on top of the lobo. Gina, the association president, stood at the stage with the scale, calling us one by one through the murmur of a large crowd.

"Jeremy Higgins." A huge crowd cheered when the vlog star walked up to the stage. They had waited through the weigh-in of a dozen other contestants to watch the new celebrity. He had become a northeastern Arizona internet sensation. He vlogged every day and hundreds were subscribing. People wanted to see him work out, eat, plan his day, and sometimes cry. The high school janitor had to roll out all their bleachers to accommodate Jeremy's fans.

He had loose skin that jiggled as he held his arms up approaching the scale. His chest and belly sagged, but I didn't worry too much, still seeing a whole bunch of fat. He had a big pair of shorts positioned just right to cover up the worst of the loose belly skin.

Lee sat with us that night. "If there were a fantasy fat loss league, I'd have drafted that kid," he said.

I leaned over to Keira. "I told you he'd be tough." She just squeezed my hand.

People cheered when they announced he'd lost thirty-two pounds and five waist sizes. The crowd fell into a throbbing chant of his name. One group tried starting a wave, but that never really made it around the bleachers.

"He does take good videos," she said.

"He does?" I asked, wondering why she was wasting her time watching him when she should have been thinking about me.

"Yeah, he shot a video of this chubby guy beating up a big lunk." She pursed her lips and talked like a baby. "It was all to protect my honor."

"Thank you for recognizing that," I said with my head held high.

She responded by digging a knuckle into my side.

"Phil Carroll," they called. Only Keira and Lee clapped. Everyone else had started leaving when Jeremy's turn ended. I walked up to the scale with my stomach somersaulting and a lump in my throat pulsing. Gina pulled a tape measure around my waist, looked at a paper on a clipboard, and announced I had lost three sizes. I felt pretty good about that, but the lump in my throat wouldn't relax until I knew what the official number was. She had me step on the scale where the red numbers flashed 216. Gina made her way back to the microphone and announced that I had lost twenty-five pounds. Only Keira's clapping echoed in the room. Lee looked bored, slouching back, leaning on the bench behind him.

As I walked back to the bleachers I froze, looking up to see Ryan slouching in the top corner. He wore a dark gray hoodie pulled low to cover the top of his face, but we still made eye contact. Not knowing what else to do, I looked up and waved at him. He shot his glance away to hide his scowl. Walking up the steps to Lee and Keira, I wondered why he had even attended. After soundly defeating the poor guy, I figured he had cleared town.

"Marty Jenkins!"

Blake left the bleachers acting like he'd never done something like this before. A few people, all wearing blue First Street Fat Loss shirts, clapped. The numbers had dwindled after Jeremy's weigh-in. Only a dozen people or so had stuck around to see the rest of the show.

"Twenty-seven pounds," Gina said into the microphone. "That places Marty in the lead, followed by Jeremy and then Phil!"

We left after Kenny Blake's numbers. Keira rubbed her hands together, biting her lower lip as we walked to the car. Her own finger drifted into the air to start her own calculations.

"Nope." I reached over, grabbing her hand and pushing it down along her side. "You don't want to open Pandora's Calculator. Just relax, we're at the midpoint. It's time to go full bore on the plan," I told her, putting my arm around her shoulder.

"You weren't going full bore?"

"No, I was. It's time for *you* to go nuts. They think I'm safely in third. It's up to Jeremy and Blake to fight me off. You talked me into turning our back on the safety net. Our backs are against the wall—"

"Sun Tzu said," Lee interrupted, "when an army feeds its horses with grain and kills its cattle for food, and when the men do not hang their cooking-pots over the camp-fires, showing that they will not return to their tents, you may know that they are determined to fight to the death."

Keira and I stopped, turning toward Lee. He shrugged with a frown. "Sun Tzu *said*."

"Killing cattle. Steak sounds good right now." I wiped some drool from the corner of my mouth.

Keira snapped at me. "Focus." Then she turned to Lee. "You, what does that have to do this?"

Lee shrugged again. "I'm just saying, you need to turn the intensity up a few clicks and fight to the death. You're really going to have to destroy Phil. Can I watch?"

I think Keira smiled at the thought of me suffering, and that hurt a little.

"Sure," she said.

"Sure me or sure him?" I asked.

"Sure," she repeated with a smirk.

Too bad we hadn't stuck around longer to watch Blake and Reggie. They were about to change everything.

***

"I found your mathlete trophy today. I cleaned out the garage," Mom said over the phone.

"Oh, great." Lying on the couch of the Bago, I thought about being a mathlete. I'd only joined because we had a chance to do the state championships at a mini-golf castle. When I arrived at the castle I didn't even try. That way I had more time to golf.

"I threw it out." She interrupted my memory.

"Oh, darn." I faked my disappointment.

"Well, if you stopped by more, you could be here to tell me about the things you want me to keep."

"That's a good point." No it wasn't. I lived in an RV. I had no choice but to own less stuff.

"So when are you leaving Arizona? It's time for me to pull out the Halloween decorations. I found some of your old costumes. Like the ghost cowboy outfit you wore that one year."

"That's right!" Now, that memory excited me. I'd had a three-piece costume for that one. I used one of those white screaming ghost masks, a cowboy vest and hat, and all black clothes underneath. When I found a house with the good candy I'd trick-or-treat as the ghost cowboy. A few minutes later I'd hide the mask in a bush. Then I'd return as a cowboy. I'd hide the vest and hat in the bushes. Then I'd return as just a ghost. I got three times the good candy with only one stop.

"Well, when are you coming home to claim your things?" she asked.

"Mom, what would you say if, by chance, I may have met a girl?"

She screamed.

Chapter 18

The days had grown shorter, and colder air started to set in. The leaves of the trees throughout the city transformed to a bright yellow that looked like lemon pie. The weather didn't matter during our workouts, since I ended up drenched in sweat every time Keira took me to exercise. It was after the workout that the cold air hurt. Walking around in a wet shirt dropped my body temperature.

"Psst!" we heard from the side of the picnic area at the park. My heart pounded from the workout, and I panted when he tried getting our attention that Friday night.

Keira and I had just finished the sixth lap of the half-mile loop around the park with exercise stations every fifty meters. Simple jogs are easy; I would just find a rhythm and stick with it. But Keira had me sprinting from station to station. I only got a minute rest in between each loop. That wouldn't have been so bad either. However, I found out that the most beautiful, intelligent, and interesting woman on the planet was also kind of mean. I'd told her to up the intensity of our program, but I think she took that as permission to yell at me more. Not a fun, motivating yell. She would call me names. Kissing me and rubbing my shoulders at the end of every workout usually helped fix that, though.

"Psst!" Jeremy tried getting our attention again. I tried to tell Keira but was gasping for air too much to talk. I could only point wildly at the bushes. She scrunched her face, failing to understand what I was doing.

"GUYS!" he finally shouted.

I didn't know who he was hiding from, but he stayed in the shadows of the ramada. Keira casually walked over to him. I fought the urge to collapse and crawl alongside her.

"I'm putting this on my vlog tonight. My, uh, friend thought you would want to know sooner," he whispered.

Jeremy held up his phone and showed us a video he'd taken. Both Reggie and Blake attacked an obstacle course. They climbed walls, crawled through mud puddles, and ran over logs. Blake helped Reggie through the course. At some of the obstacles he would bend over as a stepping stool.

The game had changed. It looked like Reggie planned on double-teaming Keira. He probably thought I was only planning on completing the mud course, not trying to win it. He was right. We had assumed that the race was just going to be between Keira and Reggie. The fight for the market was between those two; Kenny and I should have been neutral in the race. Blake helping Reggie meant that the nature of the race had changed to a team effort.

The video panned out, and to the side of the course, Ryan stood with his arms folded. He stood, blank faced, watching the two of them. Occasionally he would growl out tips on how to get past an obstacle faster.

We heard Reggie yell after straddling a wall, "Let's show these Taylor trash knuckleheads how this is done!"

When the video finished, Keira paced back and forth, swearing.

"Thanks, slim," I said, holding my cramping stomach.

Jeremy just nodded and retreated back through the shadows into the bushes. A black car rushed up, a door swung open, and Jeremy jumped in.

"Keira, it's all good," I said.

"Ryan is going to crush us!" she yelled. "He was the best person on our BattleFrog team! I was counting on Reggie not really knowing how to run an obstacle race. If Ryan is training him, he's going to be so much better than I planned."

"Okay, look on the bright side," I said, putting my hands on her shoulders. "We know now. Tomorrow, they are going to know that we know. We still have almost a month to get ready for this. They aren't going to be able to bulldoze you now that I'm going to help you through the course." I felt bad taking her in my arms with a sweaty shirt. She was sweaty too, so I hoped she wouldn't mind. I also hoped she wouldn't take in a deep breath of my aroma.

I lifted her chin with my finger. "Now, let's double what you were planning on having me do today." I frowned when she suddenly took off sprinting. I thought she would at least give me a little more time to rest.

***

The next morning, I woke up to the pounding of hammers and the shrieks of saws on wood. It was supposed to be a rest day, and all I wanted to do was sleep in. I stumbled to the front door with my eyes only half open. My hand bumped the postcard, knocking it to the floor. I glanced at it lying under the table but turned to the door.

"Why?" I shouted as I swung the door open.

Cars lined the gravel road. Dozens of men pulled logs, boards, sheets of particleboard, and tools from trailers and trucks. I recognized most of them from the ward. The rest marching past me were complete strangers.

"Mornin'!" shouted a tall bald stranger.

"Hey, Phil!" Baldini and Thompson called as they carried a big log.

The people hefted the materials to the patch of prairie across from Lee and Lizzie's house. Some had already broken up into small groups to erect walls, balance beams, and monkey bars. One group worked on a giant rope climb.

"We don't know exactly what the mud course is going to consist of, so we're just going to build everything we can think might be in it!" the bald bishop guy yelled with a saw in his hand. I jumped, turning to look down the road to where a rumble had begun. A man in a yellow hard hat drove a Bobcat loader down the road. It rolled up to a small man in an orange safety vest and began digging a small pit.

"We're going to fill that with water!" someone else I didn't know shouted. He carried a long roll of thick plastic.

I walked, in awe, across Lee's lawn in just my boxers. My mouth had fallen open watching all the people getting to work for Keira and me.

"Would you put on some pants?" Lizzie called. She, Lee, Keira, and Aiko watched the work from the porch, each holding mugs in their hands. I felt my face flush when I realized that everyone was looking at me almost in my full skin suit. I ran back to the RV to throw on some sweatpants and a shirt.

Keira handed me a mug of hot cocoa when I came back out fully clothed. We all watched the small army of workers sawing, hammering, and kicking up dust. Some people worked together perfectly. Others spent more time arguing about their project than actually building.

"So, what am I missing?" I asked.

"Let's just say they were less than excited about the video Jeremy put up last night. We citizens of Taylor don't take it very well when someone from Snowflake looks down on us," she said.

"Oh," I said. I winced a little at the searing hot cocoa.

"Why aren't you helping?" I asked Lee.

"I'm playing my 'not Mormon and not from Taylor' cards this morning," he smirked.

"Phil, come give us a hand!" Elder Thompson shouted.

I shrugged and got up. They were busy hammering a sheet of plyboard to a frame.

"We're building a wall for you to scale," Baldini said, handing me a hammer and a dozen nails. Thompson leaned over the logs, hammering everything together.

"Great." I took the nails and we began hammering the sheet to the frame. "Is this thing going to hold?" I imagined getting on top only for it to tip over.

"Yep," Thompson said. "The frame is going into a foot of concrete that Brother Hatch is going to pour. He's digging the footing now."

I looked over at a round man with a shovel digging a perfect circle. "Okay, good," I said.

"Phil," Baldini said. "Have you had a chance to think about all the stuff we talk about on our bike rides?"

"Sure." I hammered a nail in. "Why?"

"What do you think?"

"It's very complex and pretty well thought out. I guess it's all logical, if it's true."

"Have you prayed about it like we asked you to?" Thompson asked. He paused his work to look at me.

"Almost every time we see you," Baldini finished for Thompson.

167

"Pray? Well, no," I admitted. Why should I pray? Who was listening? Who cared about me enough to tell me if a book was true?

"Why not?" Baldini asked. "Just out of curiosity."

"I don't know."

"Phil, we want you to get baptized." Thompson said.

"What?" My eyes opened wide and I dropped the nails I had left.

"We've talked about baptism before. Do you remember why it is important?" Baldini asked.

"Something about a contract with Jesus. Look, I don't know that I'm the right guy for church stuff," I said, picking up the nails.

"How do you feel at church?" Thompson asked.

I could only think about Keira and sighed a little. "Good," I said.

"So, will you think about it? And then pray to know if the Book of Mormon is true and if Heavenly Father wants you to be baptized?" Baldini asked.

"Yes," I choked. "I guess I could." Thompson and Baldini smiled. They thought they hid it, but I saw them fist bump.

The bishop called me over and I helped him the rest of the morning putting up a path of balance beams.

***

Everyone finished their pieces of the course by lunch. Some of the obstacles needed a few days for the cement to dry before we could use them. Lee went into town for class and to prepare the Sushi Stop for a Saturday night.

While I helped Lizzie do the dishes from lunch and breakfast, I told her about what the missionaries had asked me to do.

"And?" she asked.

"Do you want Lee to get baptized?" I changed the subject.

"More than anything," she said, wiping a wet pan I handed her.

"Why doesn't he? He's basically a Mormon in lifestyle," I wondered.

"He hasn't heard the call, I guess," Lizzie said. She stared at a dish for a while before scrubbing it.

After we finished, I walked outside to inspect the obstacles. Keira found me casually walking over the beams that the bishop and I had set up. My arms bounced up and down trying to keep my balance. I walked one direction. She stepped up to walk the other direction. We met in the middle without a word. Keira grabbed my hands and we just looked at each other. The clouds blew by overhead, lighting and shading us. Her eyes reflected the hilly countryside behind me. She gazed up at me with a smile and leaned into me. I closed my eyes and leaned into her.

She blew in my face. My eyes popped open just as she pushed me off the beam, laughing. I tried to jump back up, but she ran off. I chased her through the course. We climbed over ladders, rolled down cargo nets, jumped over barriers. Right as I reached out for her I tripped on a rock. I yelped as I fell forward into the dirt.

I was fine, but I didn't want her to know that. Grabbing my knee, I let out a pitiful moan.

"Oh no, oh no, oh no," I whined over and over, rocking.

Keira rushed over to me and knelt at my side. Her forehead wrinkled with concern. "What happened?" she pleaded.

"I heard my knee pop," I cried, biting my lip.

She leaned over to inspect my dirty knee. That's when I reached out and I tackled her. "No!" she laughed. "You broke the honesty pact!"

Keira lay on her back with her hair splayed out over the grass and dirt. The clouds drifted by in her blue eyes. I brushed a strand of hair over her ear and watched her smile. I wanted to freeze that moment to live in it forever. The word *love* danced on my lips. Then I pulled her in for a kiss.

A solid home with a cement foundation flashed in my mind. Keira, with a kid on her lap, sat next to me on a patio while we watched the wind blow through the tall grass on the hills. A big diamond sat on her finger. A silver band wrapped around mine. I didn't worry about entry fees, prize money, or planning for what kinds of roads the Bago would fit on.

Everything suggested I should have been worried. Keira and I now had no choice but to press forward in the contest. We faced the best weight loser and the area's best trainer, and now they had a guy from the Cross Fit games on their side to coach them. But with Keira's lips on mine, I couldn't care less. I had *her*. I had her community behind us. What could go wrong?

At that moment, I should have rolled over and knocked on one of the wooden obstacles. Instead, I ran my fingers through her hair.

Chapter 19

I didn't go to the same church class with Lee and Lizzie anymore. I sat stuck in something called Gospel Principles. Lee used to go, but he'd been through it so many times that now everyone just let him go where he wanted. Keira and the missionaries made me go into a room with motivational posters for girls on the walls.

I wasn't surprised when the missionaries taught about baptism that week. I seemed to be the only person they called on to read out of the Book of Mormon. They went over why we should be baptized. They went over why in water, with authority, and by immersion. Keira would squeeze my hand to emphasize points the missionaries were making. She constantly smiled, urging me to be a part of the conversation.

I said what I thought she wanted to hear. Anything was worth seeing her smile. Her eyes would light up when I'd answer a question the right way. I understood what everyone said. I just didn't really think I wanted to do any of it. But it made her happy.

During the priesthood class I thought about it, though. I looked at Lee and thought of Lizzie. I knew they were happy. It would be hard to find a couple happier than them. They had something that I suddenly had a desire for. I thought about the previous afternoon, kissing Keira in the field. I could do this. Three-hour church had hurt at first. After I got to know everyone and they stopped treating me like an endangered species, though, it was all pretty comfortable.

After dinner that day I took Keira out to Lee and Lizzie's rocking chairs. We looked out at a sky abnormally vacant of clouds, making it huge and blue.

The white rocking chairs were side by side, rocking in unison.

"Keira?" I said confidently. I looked at her brown hair falling down her shoulders like a chocolate fountain onto a vanilla blouse. Her green skirt looked like key lime pie. She had kicked off her heels earlier, now walking around barefoot.

"Mm-hm," she said with a sigh. Her hand squeezed mine.

"I want you to know something. It's kind of a secret."

Her head turned to me. I leaned close to her, putting my other hand on top of hers. Then I whispered, "I love you."

She smiled, lifting my hand to her lips and kissing my knuckles softly. Then she leaned into my ear. "Guess what."

"What?" I turned to look at her face.

"I love you, too."

My heart jumped and I continued, "And…"

"Yes?" she whispered.

"I want to get baptized for you."

She didn't smile anymore. Instead, she confused me with a frown.

"For me?" One of her eyebrows went up, asking me to clarify.

"I'll go to church with you every week."

"For who?" she said sternly.

"Well"—my heart started pounding—"for you. Y…you seemed so happy talking to me about baptism today. I thought that becoming a Mormon would make you happy?"

172

"But it's not a decision that's supposed to be about me," she muttered, letting go of my hand. Her lips pursed and her eyebrows furrowed.

What was happening? I reviewed the last five minutes in my head. *I love you*: she accepted that and reciprocated. *I want to get baptized* got condemned? Where was I and what had suddenly happened to the woman of my dreams? She glared at me, making the world spin around me.

"You just need to figure this out," she said. "Talk to me when you get it." Keira stood up. She cracked the front door open to grab her shoes. She didn't say anything else as she walked to her car.

I ran after her. "Keira, I don't understand. Why are you mad at me?"

Her hand shot up, stopping me where I stood. "I'm . . . I'm not mad at you. *I'm* the idiot," she said, getting into her car. In less than a minute, my world flipped upside down. I felt dizzy watching her drive off. My legs couldn't take it and I collapsed next to my RV. I could only sit there with my back against my rolling house.

I sat there quiet and numb for some time—I couldn't tell how long—without any energy to even lift my wrist to look at my watch. Ants had made a trail over my legs. They weren't bothering me. Not that I would have felt them if they'd started biting. I didn't know what time it was when Lee, Lizzie, and Aiko came out. Aiko began running around the yard. Lee began rocking on the deck. Lizzie looked confused as she walked over to me.

"Phil." I just watched the hills. "Phil, honey."

"Huh?" I slowly looked up at her.

"Why are you on the ground?"

"She left."

"Who left? Keira left? I see that. What's going on?"

"I told her I loved her."

Lizzie smiled and sighed. "That's so sweet."

"And then, I told I wanted to get baptized . . ." I said, watching her smile, ". . . for her."

Lizzie's smile slowly faded and her lips turned down. "Idiot," she said as she turned and walked away.

Again, I didn't understand what had happened. Lizzie started speaking strongly to Lee. He threw his hands in the air, then he walked over to me.

"Hey, buddy," he said, sitting down next to me. "There are ants crawling on you."

"Meh," I replied.

"So things didn't go how you planned, huh?"

"No," I moaned.

"Yeah, so, do you know why I'm not a Mormon? I mean, they always talk about eternal families, and temples, and the spirit and stuff. It would blow Lizzie's mind if I got baptized."

"Well, why!" I stopped myself from shouting. "Why don't you?"

"Because it has to be for me. It has to be between God—if there is one—and me. Even though she makes me go to church, baptism is a decision that doesn't really involve Lizzie. It's my call. I need to make it when I'm ready to mean it." Lee got up. He put his hand on my shoulder, nodded, and then walked away.

I finally brushed the ants off and went to bed well past sunset. As I lay my head on the pillow I replayed the day, still not understanding why everyone was mad. Finally, I fell asleep. But I should have kept sleeping. Things didn't get any better.

***

174

Keira didn't show up the next morning. She didn't answer her phone or texts. Without anything else to do, I went to Lee's morning class with him. While I showed one of Lee's students how to pass the guard, I heard the door open and ring the bell. A stream of expletives followed and I instantly recognized Flip Gonzalo's voice. I had my back to him and all I could do was wrench my eyes shut, hoping he couldn't see my face.

"Yeah, I'm talking to you, Phil Carroll!" he yelled. "You go off showboating on the internet and you think I won't find out?"

I cringed, remembering Jeremy's video of me playing with Ryan. I hadn't thought there would be a problem, since I'd thought only people from around here watched him. Apparently he reached more than a few people in a small town in Arizona.

I turned in slow motion. The small man that we considered our jiu-jitsu system's master stood glaring at me. Flip Gonzalo's normally olive face was red. His thick finger pulled at his soul patch, dragging his bottom lip open. He wore camo cargo shorts, a plain gray t-shirt, and flip flops. Lee slouched next to him with his head down, staring at the floor.

"Get up!" he shouted. "Where's the back of this place!" Flip took off his sandals and walked across the mat. We dragged our feet following him out the back.

When the back door closed, he lit into us. I have yet to hear a more colorful and creative use of profanity. His time as a Marine Corps drill instructor manifested in his rage and his trembling frame. Spit flew as he shook his arms and pointed his fingers at us. I was afraid to look at him. At one point I expected a blood vessel in his eye to break, but I was too scared to look.

After about ten minutes of screaming, he finally seemed to calm down. "Don't you have a class to teach?" he hissed at Lee.

Lee just nodded. He ran back inside, leaving me to the little demon man. I finally looked up from the ground to find a cold stare from his light brown eyes and flaring nostrils.

"Do you want back in?" he asked quietly.

"Yes, sir." I muttered.

"Then you're coming with me. I hear you have a motorhome?"

"Yes, but—"

He cut me off. "Meet me in Phoenix tonight. I'm dropping off my rental and you are coming back to Southern California to earn your way back in."

"I want to so bad, but—"

He just flashed a look of rage at me again. I shut up. "You're going to give me three weeks. I am going to slay you."

My finger went in the air. Three weeks? The final weigh-in and the race would be in four. I had time. My hand ran through my hair. That gave me no time to train with Keira. If she even wanted to train with me.

Flip swung the door open and walked through Lee's class. He stopped at the front door and turned around to speak to the innocent students. "I love that you are learning from Lee and chose my system. I'm sorry I can't stay longer." He pointed at Lee. "I have something planned for you. Always train your hardest, BE HONEST, and don't be stupid." He pushed the door and left.

Lee looked at me. I shrugged and pushed out the door to walk back home. Flip was being generous to let me fight my way back in. I believed him that he was going to "slay" me, though. I remembered the stories he used to tell about torturing Marine recruits. I imagined being face-down in sand, doing push-ups while he kicked more sand on me.

Instead of immediately walking home, I drifted over to the Sushi Stop. The door of course was closed, but I could see Uncle Tim sweeping the floor. I pounded on the door to get his attention and he smiled at seeing me.

"Phil, it's early," he said, opening the door.

"I know, *oji*. I just need to take care of the tree for now. I'll be gone for a while."

"Gone? Why? Who's going to take care of that stupid thing?" He pointed at the bonsai, then resumed sweeping while I sat at the bar to begin trimming the bonsai.

"Well, I guess you or Lee will need to."

"I've really liked my reprieve from gardening."

"I know, I'm sorry. I'll only be gone for three weeks."

"Where?"

"Back to California to get back in with Flip and the system."

"What about the contest? What about Keira?"

Then I thought about Keira. Would she think I'd abandoned her? How could I explain what I was doing? She knew how much this would mean to me. I had to try to talk to her first. I tried calling, but she didn't answer so I just left a message.

"Hey, so I'm sorry I didn't understand this whole baptism thing. I have a slight problem. I will be here for you. I'll be at the weigh-in and will do everything in my power to help you win the race. Uh, there's one problem. I'll be gone for a few weeks. Lee will tell you what happened. I'll call you every night and report what I've done during the day. Don't worry about my diet or exercise. Someone already has that planned out. I do love you."

Uncle Tim moved to the back of the bar, where he fished out a couple of celery sticks for me. "So, was that what all the yelling was about outside? Me and the boys could hear everything from the kitchen."

"Yeah, Flip just left. I've got a chance to get back in. I could still go to Japan, get my affiliation with Flip, and finally find a place to settle."

"You can't settle here, can you?"

"No, not with Lee so close. I'd have to find somewhere outside of some radius that Flip determines."

"But Keira won't leave Taylor?"

"No, but she's mad at me right now. Plus, what does that matter?"

"You want to be together."

"Well, I want to be with her."

"But your plans will force you apart?"

"Plans?"

"You're getting married, right? I mean, Mormons marry fast, don't they?"

"Marriage! We've barely been dating!"

"But you've spent almost every day with her for a month, right?"

"I guess so, but come on, marriage?" Sure, the thought had crossed my mind just two days before. But that was just a brief thought. Why was Tim bringing up the *M* word? I got so worked up thinking about it that I over-snipped and felled a large branch of the small tree. We both cursed, looking at the odd shape of part of the tree. I handed the scissors over to Uncle Tim, who gave me a full bag of celery stalks.

"Hang on," he grunted, then finally said it. "*Oi*."

I gasped. "You did it. You called me nephew."

"Don't dwell on it. Look, you take that piece of junk with you. Take care of it out there and bring it back in one piece. I'll give you a ride back to Lee's.

My new *oji* dropped me off at my Winnebago. I strapped some of my stuff down in the house and then pulled the blocks from the wheels to head out after leaving one more goodbye message on Keira's voicemail.

Chapter 20

Early the next morning, we left the hotel by the Phoenix airport where he'd stayed the night. I'd stayed in a Wal-Mart parking lot and picked him up at the break of dawn. Flip made the ride from Phoenix to Santa Ana, California one long lecture. Flip went on and on about honesty.

"No one will ever trust me or my work based on your dishonesty. You think I'm the only one that noticed you and Lee weren't really fighting at that tournament? Everyone there with experience knew what you were doing. Sure, some of the new people couldn't see it. Even if other experts didn't see it, I saw it. How am I supposed to build a system if I'm accused of setting my students up to throw matches?

"I just thought—" I started.

"You thought about yourself."

"No, I thought about you. I thought about helping Lee. What was I going to gain?"

Flip just looked out the window at the desert passing by.

"I guess you're right about that. But I'd have preferred to have seen thirty seconds of you really trying compared to four minutes of you holding back."

"You're not very good at this mysterious master thing. Aren't you supposed to tell me to snatch something from your hand or something?"

"What I have is going to be much worse for you," he said with a smile. "It's almost the same thing I did to Lee when he wanted back in. After he came and apologized, of course. You tried training through deception. So it will be worse for you."

I started to panic as he continued with his lecture. Lee had never told me what he'd actually had to do. He only ever told me that he went through a lot to end his jiu-jitsu banishment. Pushing that aside, I thought about Keira. Maybe this would be for the best. If I could get back in with Flip, I could settle down somewhere. Hopefully become an instructor. Maybe I could settle down with her. She was a trainer. I'd be an instructor. We could go anywhere and do anything.

***

The next three weeks were as terrible as he'd promised. I'd assumed Flip would squeeze everything out of me. He went much further than I anticipated. We didn't just visit all his affiliates in Southern California. I'd show up at the gym hours before he did and clean the place for the owner. Then I'd roll with the owner, who I think had specific instructions to go hard on me. I would participate in every class that whole day. Flip would stop by or call at some point and tell me where to go the next day. At the end of the day I'd clean the owner's gym again. Every day I had a place to stop and prove myself.

Flip put me through a grueling routine, but the owners were at least kind. Most expressed that they were glad it was happening to me and not them. At one point, others had thought of doing what Lee and I had pulled off. When all the other members of Flip's system saw what happened to me, they were glad to see the consequences of fudging the results of matches. They didn't go easy on me, though. The last part of my training day I always faced each head instructor at the gym.

Just two days in and I hated every life decision I had ever made. I lay in bed hungry, sore, and willing Keira to call me back. I would end every day by calling to give her a report of what I'd eaten and how I'd trained. Every break, time out, and bathroom run I took, I hoped to see a call or a text from her. Nothing. My heart hurt more than my sore body.

For all I knew, everything had fallen apart. Reggie had probably already run Keira out of town. She'd probably found solace in Ryan's arms. Blake probably thought he could start counting his cash. *Stupid me*, I kept telling myself.

When I walked into the RV one of those nights, I hurled my shoes across the living space. They crashed against a shelf and the Book of Mormon fell onto the leather couch. I marched over to it. I stared at it, thinking all my problems were because of this dumb book. I just about threw it across the room too. Before I could, something just broke.

I fell to my knees. I looked at the book with disdain. Why was this so important? I was willing to go to church with her. Who cared if it was true or not? Why was it important if I believed? I wanted to support her! I nearly screamed.

I got up and lay on the couch with the book on my chest. Keira's face filled my mind as I flipped through the pages, seeing all the notes and parts she had marked for me. Regardless of all those notes, I opened the book and started at the beginning. It took some time, but I finally found the first chapter. I read for almost an hour about the guy Nephi and his dad Lehi.

The difficulty of my new routine shifted my mindset. I don't know why, but when you spend an hour or two cleaning, another eight to ten hours protecting yourself from chokes and arm locks, and then another two cleaning again, you fall into a state of contemplation. With so much reflection, the book became interesting.

After a day of thinking about what I'd read, I pulled out my phone.

"Yeah, Baldini, this is Phil."

"Hey, Phil, Sister Akiyama told us you'd be gone for a while," he said.

"Yeah, sorry, I'll be doing some business in California for a few weeks. I have a question. When did all of this Book of Mormon stuff take place?" I asked.

"Well, if you just look at the bottom of the page——-"

I cut him off. "The bottom corner of the page? Oh, look at that. So this Nefey guy knew about Jesus before Jesus was born? I mean, I assume he's talking about Jesus when he talks about a messiah, right?"

"Phil, it's Nephi——-go to the very last part of the book. Look for the pronunciation guide."

"Pronunciation guide?" I flipped through the book. "Well, how about that. So how did he know about Jesus?"

"All the prophets do," he answered.

"They all knew about Jesus? Okay. Well I'm going to keep reading . . . good night."

"Night, Phil." We hung up.

I opened the book again to continue.

One night I got to the section where the converted bad guys wouldn't fight after the Ammon guy baptized them. What the heck? An army came specifically to kill them and they just let them?

> *Alma 24:13 Behold, I say unto you, Nay, let us retain our swords that they be not stained with the blood of our brethren; for perhaps, if we should stain our swords again they can no more be*

*washed bright through the blood of the Son of our
great God, which shall be shed for the atonement
of our sins.*

The "Son of our great God" I assumed to be Jesus.
My finger went in the air, now calculating the cost of sin.
Their swords were stained with blood, then they got
baptized and their swords lost their stains because they
were washed in the blood of Jesus. If they stained them
again, they were afraid that they wouldn't be able to get
the stain out. So these people would rather die than break
their promise with God? My finger fell. That seemed like
a good deal.

The next day I kept thinking about it. At some point
someone had my arm stretched out in an arm bar, but I
was still thinking of dirty swords. That night I called the
missionaries again while I tended to the bonsai.

"Thompson?" I asked. The voice sounded different.

"No, sorry, he's been transferred," the voice said.

"Oh, he's been transferred? ... So who is this?" I
asked.

"This is Elder White. I'm new, but Elder Baldini is
still here."

"Okay, well, Elder White, I'm Phil Carroll and I have
a question for you. How did Jesus wash the bad guys'
swords?"

"Who?"

"The people Ammon baptized," I asked.

"Well, they repented and made a new covenant with
him," he said.

"But they still killed people in the past, so how do
they reverse that?" I muttered.

"Jesus took upon him our sins. So he forgives us."

"Jesus just forgave them?"

"He can forgive all of us, including you."

"Well, I hope he'd forgive me; I've never done anything as bad as killing anyone," I said.

"Perfect, that hope is good," he informed me.

"Oh, hope is good?"

"Phil, would you mind if I had you skip ahead to a part of the book that might answer some questions?" he asked.

"Skip ahead? Well, I guess so."

"I'd like you to go to the Book of Moroni and reach chapter seven, verse forty," he suggested.

"Okay. Tell Baldini that Phil says hi. Thank you, goodbye."

Skip ahead? Fine.

I turned the pages to Moroni seven.

> *Moroni 7:40 And again, my beloved brethren, I would speak unto you concerning hope. How is it that ye can attain unto faith, save ye shall have hope?*

I did just tell the new kid that I would hope Jesus would forgive me. But forgive me for what? Well, I wasn't perfect. Maybe I wasn't always honest. If there was a guy in heaven who was going to grant me some sort of rest, would he want me to be honest?

The next day as I was wiping up and sterilizing a small pool of blood, I kept thinking about it. Someone's elbow had smashed into his opponent's forehead and created a geyser. The gym owner had me go over the whole mat just to be safe. As I poured some bleach on the spot, I thought about whether I had been honest. I didn't feel very good about myself.

That night I continued reading. Elder White had given me permission to skip to the end, so I went on. In the next chapter, I found that the Moroni guy was talking about how I was feeling.

> *Moroni 8:26 And the remission of sins bringeth meekness, and lowliness of heart; and because of meekness and lowliness of heart cometh the visitation of the Holy Ghost, which Comforter filleth with hope and perfect love, which love endureth by diligence unto prayer, until the end shall come, when all the saints shall dwell with God.*

I guess I wanted perfect love. I mean, who didn't want perfect love? Even Keira couldn't give *perfect* love. I certainly couldn't. That sounded pretty good. If all this Mormon stuff was true and following it I could get perfect love from a perfect being, why wouldn't I want that?

Flipping the pages, I found dozens of marks. Keira had been through it with a pen and circled and underlined a bunch of things. The part most highlighted was the part that said, *sincere heart, with real intent, having faith in Christ.*

Well, those were pretty convenient qualifiers. I pulled out my phone.

"Baldini!" I shouted with him on speaker as I trimmed the bonsai. "What does Moroni mean by 'real intent'?"

"Why do you want to know if this is true, and what is your intent if he reveals that it is true?" his voice replied.

"So God will answer me only if I really *intend* to follow him if he answers me? Fine. I'm pretty sure I'll be back sometime next week."

"Good night, Phil."

The next week I thought about real intent. When I was mopping up puke, sweat, and blood I'd think about my own state and if I really intended to do what God would want. While someone was choking me or attacking my joints, I thought about my original intent and how it was only to please Keira. It had nothing to do with even trying to know God.

Finally, my three weeks were over. I was exhausted but felt strong. When I had first arrived, those fifteen-minute rounds rolling against all the instructors were hell on Earth. As the weeks went by, I was able to last longer and even fight back instead of just defend.

I received a text from flip.

Your last night is tomorrow. Meet me at HQ in the morning.

I was with Galileo that night. He was a large Mexican with muscles on muscles. We called him Galileo because of the moves he invented. I'd almost finished mopping his mats when I got the text. I called him over and told him.

"Congrats, man," he said. "Flip called a few of us black belts to meet with him and with you tomorrow."

"What are you going to do?"

"Consider it a, um, trial? Yeah man, a trial," he said. "So the UFC fight is tonight, wanna come with us? A bunch of my students are going to a sports bar."

"Yeah, sure," I said, finishing my tasks in his gym. The Santa Ana HQ was pretty close by. I didn't have far to travel in the morning.

An hour later we found a spot at a forgettable sports bar. There were a bunch of televisions in all the corners of the small bar. Bottles and glasses were clinking. The smell of deep-fried food drifted from the kitchen. People milled around carrying their drinks, laughing and shouting. Since it was fall, most of the TVs had on some college football game.

Galileo's students and I occupied a corner where one small TV showed the fight. They were drinking and eating, while I had a bag of celery and a glass of light beer someone had bought for me. I sat aloof, twirling the suds around without drinking.

Everyone around me cheered, told dirty jokes, drank, and ate. The waitresses were dressed as referees. Their striped shirts were very tight and very low. They didn't wear much over their legs, just short black skirts.

Then a chair squealed when someone dragged it over to sit down next to me. An insanely pretty redheaded girl smiled at me. She wore a low-cut tank top. Her legs were hardly covered by her cut-offs. She had blue eyes and soft, milky skin. When she smiled, there were two small dimples on her cheeks.

"Hi," she said.

I looked around to see who she was talking to.

She put her hand on my leg. "Hi," she said again, looking in my eyes.

"Oh, hello," I said. My face felt warm. Even though I'd showered at Galileo's gym, I felt disheveled, grimy, and tired. I hadn't assumed this redheaded bombshell was talking to me.

"I'm a friend of one of Galileo's students' girlfriends."

The crowd around us roared. We both turned to the TV, which replayed a nasty knockout.

"I'm sorry, what?"

"I'm a friend of one of Galileo's students' girlfriends," she repeated.

"So, what does that make us?" I smiled.

She put her hand on my shoulder and laughed. "That's so funny, I guess nothing yet."

Yet? I looked around. Everyone around me indulged in the life the bar offered. The barely-clothed waitresses bounced from table to table. There were sticky spots on the floor where drinks had spilled. A group of women was dancing in a corner.

"Well, I'm just visiting. I'll be gone tomorrow," I told her.

"Oh, that's too bad. I know all of Galileo's group. I figured I'd talk to you, since you seem a little more down to earth," she said. Her hand lingered on my shoulder, shooting a chill down my spine.

"What does that mean?" I asked.

"Listen to all these guys. Choke this, takedown that. You'd think there was nothing in this world but grappling and fighting." She pouted with her lips.

"I'd probably be saying the same thing; I'm just really tired," I said, looking at the TV.

"Why?"

"I've just been traveling a lot recently."

"Oh, well maybe we could go somewhere else?" She tugged a little on my sleeve.

"Like where?"

"Just a street over. They have an art walk," she suggested. "My place isn't far either." Her hand ran back down my arm to my leg.

I used to jump at the chance to hang out with friends at a bar and meet new women. I'd loved sports bars with friends, beer, and fried food. Now I looked at the woman whose name I didn't know, less than dressed, practically begging me to go out with her. And not just go out with her, but to *go* out with her. Even with all of that right at the tips of my fingers, it didn't feel happy.

What was wrong with me? I just spun the beer froth in circles, still not tasting it. Nothing about this place filled the hole that a lack of Keira had punched in my heart. With all the commotion around me, I thought about only her.

I leaned back in my chair, closing my eyes, not caring about the girl touching me. My mind set the stage of the perfect moment. I imagined walking with Keira in the gold waving grass of the hills by Lee and Lizzie's. My mind made it sunset. The clouds towered in the sky, deep purple, pink, and yellow. We walked hand in hand. The wind flowed through her dark, silky hair. I imagined a perfectly set log where we sat down. She slipped her hand into mine, resting her head on my shoulder. I froze the image, and the last thing that Uncle Tim had talked to me about ran through my mind.

A clatter of plates woke me up. I tried to close my eyes again, but I'd lost the image. The redheaded girl had her hand in mine.

Something clicked. Nothing here would make me happy.

"Look," I said, letting go of her hand. "I don't have a job and I live in a motorhome."

"Um, okay?"

I just waved to Galileo. I felt no regret as I left. After only a short walk down the block to where I'd left the RV, I drove it straight to the empty parking lot of Flip's HQ.

I lay in bed thinking about everything. Nothing at that bar could compare to even the goofy, cheesy Victory Dance. Even though I'd sulked most of that night, it had felt different. The two environments were incomparable. I used to think I could have real fun at the bar. How did the Mormons have fun without all the things that the rest of us think we have to have in order to have fun?

Finally I fell asleep, able to find the imagined sunset with Keira again.

***

Flip had made his headquarters out of a small furniture sales room he had repurposed into his gym. Large U.S. and Brazilian flags hung from the largest wall, with smaller flags from various countries where he had an affiliate hanging under them. The walls were lined with green vinyl padding up to about three feet and mirrors another three feet. Three-row bleachers lined his huge mat space.

Flip and five other men kneeled in front of me on the mat. I kneeled facing them. The others were the closest black belts who operated nearby. One was a tall black man with a bushy black beard and a shaved head. Next to him was Galileo, the chiseled Mexican I'd been with the night before. Two smiling white guys were identical twins with buzzed heads and deep dimples when they smiled. Behind them were fifteen students.

"You're going to roll with each of us for three minutes, meaning you're going to roll for an hour straight. You don't get a break. You'll begin and end with me."

I just nodded, and the worst hour of my life began. I didn't have the skill to match the black belts. Even their students were good. I only tried to fend them off. The last three weeks were good for getting me in grappling shape, but after eight opponents, I wanted to quit. The tall black guy used his legs like a second set of arms. Instead of fighting against two hands I fought against four. He could hook anything he wanted with his feet. I kept backing up, trying to find the right time to shoot in on one of those strong limbs..

"Endure, Phil!" Flip shouted. "Up, up, up!"

I grappled through three more students, able to dominate only one. He had a weak guard I could easily pass. When I controlled his side I took a moment to catch a breath. I think Flip could tell I tried resting when I stopped attempting anything and just sucked in deep breaths as I hunched over my opponent. He switched out the student with a new one who came forward, judo tossing me. We'd rolled for a minute when he spun over me, finding my arm. Within a matter of seconds he hyperextended it.

I must have been on my last ten minutes. Flip called everyone to step back. He crouched, waiting for me to attack when I staggered to my feet. I could only stumble forward with my hands out and my head falling forward. He pushed it away with a laugh. I turned to follow him, grunting and panting. I threw my arms up to try to catch him. Everyone joined him in laughing.

"Zombie offense," someone shouted.

"All right!" Flip called to me. He walked over to me, lightly slapping me on the face. "It's over." With that permission, I collapsed. "THAT! That right there. *That's* how I want to see you when you compete. I want to know that you left everything on the mat! I don't care about fancy technique. I want to know that whether you win or lose, you left it all out there like a samurai, like a cherry blossom!"

I lay on my back, staring at the ceiling. A pair of blue eyes blocked out the florescent lights above me. The light around her head made her look like an angel. My heart already pounded through my chest. I was completely out of breath. Despite all of that, I gasped and my heart fluttered.

I tilted my head and furrowed my eyebrows. "Did I die?" I asked.

"Nope," Keira said with a smile.

***

Everyone had found space on the mat and were now rolling with each other. Keira sat next to me as I held a bag of ice on my ear.

"Why are you here? I thought you hated me," I said to her.

"Hate you?" she said.

"You wouldn't talk to me."

"Lee said –"

"Lee? What did Lee say?" I growled.

"Lee said that he'd been through this before and that it was best not to have any distractions. He'd been keeping tabs with Flip and asked if I wanted to come out. Lizzie wanted me to come out and surprise you. Flip picked me up at the airport. We had lunch and he told me what he was going to do. He's such a nice guy."

I didn't know what to say.

Keira pointed at me. "I wanted this for you. I didn't want to be in the way. Lee said how much it would mean to you if I came tonight."

"I couldn't have asked for more," I said. "I thought about you so much."

"Oh really?" Her eyes dropped to the bench in front of us.

"Well, maybe just a little," I laughed.

"So," she started.

"So?" I looked into her eyes.

"So . . . um . . ."

The benches creaked as Flip and Galileo walked over to us.

"Did you enjoy yourself?" Flip asked.

"No," I said.

"I was talking to Keira," he replied, looking past me to her.

"Your place is fantastic," she said.

"I knew there was a girl," Galileo said.

"What do you mean?" Keira asked.

"We went and watched the fight last night at a bar close to my place. This hot girl was just about to crawl all over him."

Keira flashed me a look. She went red and her nose flared. Why didn't he start with the end of the story?

"Out of nowhere, Phil just leaves," Galileo finished.

The edge of her lips curled up just a little.

"I hear you're going back to Arizona to finish your marketing plan for Keira," Flip said.

"Yep," I smiled.

"Well, I'm going to need you to be ready at some point. I have something planned for Lee."

"But I thought he was okay?" I asked.

"No, I banned you. Everyone was under strict orders not to train you."

"Flip, it's my fault. I leveraged his family to get him to help me. You punished the right person." I looked down at the bench in front of me.

"That's no excuse. He was at fault those years ago when you faked the match and threw the tournament as much as he is now. Lee is the best teacher I have. But for some reason he has a soft spot for you, and you

194

manipulate him at will. I want you spending time with him to learn the ropes. Go back and tell him to expect me to call on him when he least expects it. So go on, get outta here."

Keira followed me out to the Bago and I drove her to the nearest hotel. I walked her to the door, where she quickly gave me a peck on the cheek and disappeared behind the door.

I drove off to find the last Wal-Mart parking lot I'd have to park in for some time.

Chapter 21

Keira and I drove eight and a half hours from Santa Ana, California to Taylor. She just watched the road go by in silence. A few times she sat up straight, about to say something. Then she slouched back down in the chair. I just wanted her by my side and didn't care about the silence. I loved looking over at her, one leg tucked under her while she hugged the other knee.

She counted it all as a rest day when we rolled back into Lee and Lizzie's driveway. No workout waited for me when I got home. Keira left me to settle back in and tend to my bruises from the trial.

Lizzie was glad I was back. Actually, she wasn't glad that I was back so much as she was glad she could leave Aiko with me. Almost as soon I got back, she ran to the store and I watched Aiko play in the yard while I rocked on the porch with the Book of Mormon.

It had gotten a lot colder. Our breaths shot out in puffs. She was bundled in a thick hooded coat and warm fleece pants. I just had on a sweater and jeans. My fingers were cold enough that I had to switch hands every few minutes and stick them under my shirt. I gave up when Aiko began to sing a song about trying to be like Jesus.

While she sang, I read in the Book of Moroni. I felt drawn to look down at the pages.

> *Moroni 7:13 But behold, that which is of God inviteth and enticeth to do good continually; wherefore, every thing which inviteth and enticeth to do good, and to love God, and to serve him, is inspired of God.*

I felt warm. I didn't want to hesitate anymore. With Aiko singing, I kneeled on the hard patio. I spoke to whoever listened. I told him I wanted to do what *He* wanted. It didn't really matter what Keira wanted. More importantly, I didn't care what I wanted anymore. My dream trip to Japan, my own school, none of that mattered as I spoke. The warmth spread through me as I prayed. No one spoke to me; there weren't angels; I only felt . . . perfect love.

When I finished, Aiko stood next to me smiling. Tears rolled down my cheeks. She wiped one away.

"It's okay, Uncle Phil."

"Yeah, it is," I said, pulling out my phone.

"Elder White? . . . Yeah, this is . . . Yes, I'm back in town . . . Can you two come over? . . . Okay, I'll see you soon."

I took Aiko inside and waited for the missionaries. She was playing with Legos when they finally arrived. We sat on the couch and watched Aiko tinker with the bricks. Baldini asked me questions about California and my sudden departure. Elder White just watched me. His skin, hair, and eyes were very dark.

Elder White jumped in when I'd caught them up on what had happened. "Phil, not to be curt, but why did you call us over?"

"I'm ready to be baptized," I said.

"Why?" he asked.

"*I* want to make a contract with God." my voice trembled a little.

He looked at me sternly. "Sister Brimhall told us about your last conversation about baptism."

"And now I want to, for Him, and for me," I said.

Elder White smiled and asked, "What happened?"

We spoke about what had happened just a half hour before. They taught me about the Holy Ghost, more about baptism, and what was expected after. I wanted to join the church as soon as possible. They looked at me a little funny when I told them I wanted it that Friday night. I had been to church a number of times, and they didn't see any reason why I couldn't. They promised to have someone come talk to me soon.

A knock at the door interrupted us. I opened the door to find Lizzie waiting to get in with arms full of grocery bags.

"Whoa!" she cried when the missionaries rushed up to help her in. They told us to sit at the counter, and then ran back and forth from her kitchen to the car, bringing in all the bags. I did my best to put the food where it belonged. She munched on an apple, directing me where to put her groceries away. When we finished, the missionaries told me they'd see me in a couple of days.

"What are you doing in two days?" she asked when they left.

"Well, some other missionary is going to come over and give me some sort of interview."

"Interview?" Her eyebrows shot up.

"Yes?" I said smiling. I sat next to her and grabbed an apple.

"No way!" she slapped my arm really hard. "Wait, why?"

"I promise that it has nothing to do with your sister, you, or the pope."

"So?" she asked.

"I'm going to be baptized on Friday night."

"Oh my gosh, I'm going to need to make cookies!" she jumped up and ran to her cupboards to look at her ingredients.

"There's something else," I said.

"Yes?" she said with her back to me.

"Um, do you know where I can get a ring?"

Something crashed to the floor. I saw shards of glass and cinnamon all over the floor.

"What did you say?" she squealed.

"A ring?" I asked again.

"Sweep a path for me. I've got something for you."

I ran to the side of the fridge where she kept the broom. She watched me intently as I began sweeping around her feet so she didn't step on loose shards. When I had cleared the floor she ran down the hall to her room. I heard shuffling, cursing, and things falling. The cinnamon puffed into a cloud when I dumped it in the trash.

"I found it!" she yelled from her room. "I forgot where I hid it, but I found it!" She walked down the hall holding her arm up triumphantly. Something sparkled in her hand.

She held out a simple, underwhelming gold ring with a tiny diamond in it.

"Wow, Lizzie," I said with a forced smile. "Well, I was, uh, thinking of getting something a little bigger."

"No," she demanded.

"Wel—"

"You are going to give her this ring. It's the ring our grandfather gave to our grandmother when he returned from Vietnam. She's always wanted this ring. My grandmother gave it to Lee instead, to give to me. Last year he got me a new one. I would have given it to Keira, but she was divorced by then. So now it's her turn. You are going to propose with this ring."

"Yes, ma'am." I smiled thinking of kneeling in front of Keira.

"Now, go do something while I plan your proposal."

"Can't I plan my own—" She cut me off again with a snap.

"No!" she said and went into the kitchen.

"Hey, Lizzie." I followed her in.

"Yeah?" she tapped and scrolled on her phone.

"Why were you mad at me the night before I left?"

"*Mad* at you?"

"And I quote, 'idiot.' That's the last thing you said to me before I left."

Lizzie laughed. "No, I didn't call you an idiot. I called Keira an idiot."

"Why?"

"When she first told me that the missionaries had asked you about baptism, I warned her to back off a little and leave it between you and them. But she didn't listen."

"So you're not mad?"

"No, why?"

"You're terrifying when you're angry."

"Just go, I have your proposal to plan."

***

I did just what Lizzie told me to do. All I had to do was walk Keira up the same hill we'd run up the first time she'd worked out with me at sunset. Lizzie had more going on. She spoke on the phone all the next day getting things ready. Before Keira showed up, she disappeared with Aiko.

That afternoon we were dressed casually. I just wore a green sweater, khaki shorts, and my beat-up old running shoes with a toe popping out. Keira wore blue jeans and a thick flannel jacket. Her hair fell down both of her shoulders.

"I don't have a real workout planned for you."

That worked out, because Lizzie expected me at the top of the hill soon.

"Let's walk up our hill," I suggested as we reached the pavement. My hand hid in the pocket of my shorts, fumbling with the ring.

"I want you to take it easy," she said, pulling me the opposite way.

"I, uh, don't want to take it easy," I protested.

"You're still delirious. You need to take it easy, just tonight."

"No," I said pulling her toward the hill. I looked at the sky—the sun would be setting some time in the next forty minutes.

"Yes," she pulled back.

"Please, please just come with me up the hill. I'll go slow, but not too slow."

She rolled her eyes. "Fine," she relented. Then, "Why are you hands so sweaty?"

"I just, I'm having a flashback to all the suffering I went through with Flip?"

"Are you asking me or telling me?"

"Telling you."

"You poor baby," she said, wrapping her arm around mine.

"What's going on up there?" she asked when we were just about to reach the top.

I panted . . . I hadn't lost my ability to walk uphill. The three weeks at sea level had ruined my lungs again. I put my hands over my head when we reached the top.

Lizzie's surprise waited for us. A flatbed trailer parked along the side of the road. A brunette girl held a guitar. Next to her a pimply teenage boy waited with a snare drum. He held one drumstick, one of those wire ones that looked like a brush. By the drummer stood another girl, plump and redheaded, with a ukulele.

The brunette began to sing the old Louis Armstrong "Wink and a Smile" song. Lizzie held Aiko behind the flatbed. She stared at me. When we made eye contact her eyebrows shot up. "Ask her!" she mouthed.

While the girl kept singing, I got down on a knee. "Keira Brimhall . . ."

Keira pulled me to my feet. "Phil . . . I . . . no."

A wild twang echoed through the hills when one of the guitar strings snapped. I had to look around at everyone else. Lizzie's mouth fell wide open. The small band looked at one another. The singer stared at the drummer, who had his shoulders up. The ukulele player slowly rested the instrument in its case.

"Phil, I'm sorry, I just can't." She turned and ran down the hill.

***

I walked for about an hour. Lizzie tried saying something to me when I left. All I could hear was muffled sound at that point. Just as the last purple glow in the west disappeared, I found my way back to Lee's house.

I found Lee leaning against the hood of his car, his headlights shining on the obstacle course where someone ran around. He had a plate in his hand with a roll of sushi that he picked at with chopsticks.

"Congratulations!" he said, chewing on rice and raw fish. I saw that it was Jeremy who ran through the course.

He looked skinny now in the glow of the headlights. He ran at the wall, but couldn't jump up high enough to climb it. I looked around, wondering why I didn't see anyone with any type of recording device.

"Yeah, not so much," I said. "So what's with Jeremy?" I wanted to change the subject.

Lee pursed his lips, looking at me sideways. He was going to probe more. I looked at him, biting hard into my lower lip. My eyes blinked back tears, but only because of the pollen in the air. He frowned, swallowing his mouthful of rice and fish. "He's worried about the race on Saturday."

"He looks pretty slim."

"Worried?"

"A little. But look at this," I said raising my shirt. "You can see my ribs. I figure he has some loose skin still weighing him down." My belly looked pretty loose too, but not like Jeremy's.

Lee just grunted.

We watched Jeremy try a few more times. He gave up and hobbled over to us. His cheeks had become bright red blotches.

"I'm in trouble," he said.

"Nah," Lee told him. "You just need a few inches to get your hand up there. Do you have tall shoes?"

"Very funny," the kid said. Jeremy turned to me. "So, you got released from the North Korean prison camp you were in, Mr. Ribs?"

Lee almost choked on his last piece of sushi. "Nice burn!" he said, bumping Jeremy's fist.

My face became warm, probably turning as red as his.

"Can you parachute with that loose skin?" I muttered. I wanted someone else to hurt with me.

"Wow," he said lifting his shirt. His skin was so loose it was like a drape. "With these abs? I've got three girls."

Lee looked at me. "I've seen them."

"Fine," I moaned and went to bed.

Chapter 22

I didn't tell many people about my baptism.

The church was warm with the smell of Lizzie's snickerdoodles floating through the halls. Before the service, everyone loitered next to the kitchen. The bishop, the missionaries, and the few members of the ward that the missionaries insisted should be there were waiting for the water to fill up in another room. They had followed the smell of cookies while they waited.

I thought back on my conversation with the missionary who'd given me the interview. All his questions had been pretty easily answered. One thing kept nagging at me. I had told him everything. I'd told him why exactly I traveled to Taylor and that I wasn't really who I made myself out to be.

He had just smiled.

"When's the last time you wrote a fake review?" he asked.

"Not since I went to California," I told him.

He smiled again. "Just be honest. I feel that you are ready to make a covenant with the Lord. If there is anyone that you feel you need to tell, then do it quickly."

My heart thumped in my chest as I looked at everyone drooling over the cookies. "Everyone, I need to tell you something about me," I said, interrupting their conversation.

The group took their eyes off the cookies and looked at me.

I tugged at my collar. "I'm not really who I pretended to be when I got here." Lee and Lizzie glanced at each other, then looked at me nervously.

"Your name *is* Phil Carroll, right?" the bishop asked.

"Yes, but I came here with the sole purpose of winning the prize tomorrow."

"Okay, so?" the ward mission leader asked. He rubbed his big meaty hands on his face.

"So, I wasn't really here to lose weight. I just followed the prize money. I don't really live here. I hadn't ever intended on staying."

"Don't you have an Arizona driver's license?" Lee said. He knew full well that I did.

"Yes, but that's not the point."

"You plan on staying," the bishop said.

"I was."

"Our driveway is open to you for as long as you need," Lizzie said.

"You're making the right decisions now. Tonight is about starting a new life. Don't worry about the past," the bishop said.

"Oh. Well then, let's get baptized," I said. "The smell of those cookies is killing me."

Minutes later, we sat in one of the side rooms that I didn't know about, singing a hymn. I sat in a white jumpsuit with Aiko on my lap. Elder Baldini sat next to me in white pants, a white tie, and his normal white shirt.

Lee and Lizzie were behind us. Lee looked like a Mormon in a full suit. Lizzie constantly had a tissue to her eyes, wiping away tears.

Someone gave a short talk. The same girl who sang when I failed my proposal sang a beautiful song about something churchy. Then the bishop asked Baldini and me to get in the water. It was all surreal. The warm water went up to my waist. Baldini said something and then I went under the water.

Later, after changing, the bishop and the missionaries put their hands on my still-wet head. For all the emphasis on doing these things, there was very little ceremony to it, but something about it all felt right.

After the service ended, Lizzie put me through pure torture. Everyone ate those sweet cinnamon-smelling snickerdoodles after the service. Someone brought a small vegetable platter for me on the side. Lizzie threw out the ranch dip. I imagined my celery was a soft mound of cookie covered in cinnamon. It didn't work.

"What's going on?" Keira's voice sounded stunned.

Everyone's eyes went wide. I still crunched on a mouthful of not-snickerdoodle. I turned around. Keira wore a college t-shirt and jeans. Her pants were rolled up mid-calf, showing some of her caramel skin. She wore red flip-flops that matched freshly manicured toes the color of pizza sauce. I assumed she'd wanted to relax the night before the race. She had gone a step further with her chocolate hair, and each side of her head had two cornrows she'd pulled back with the rest of her hair in a ponytail.

"Hi-oh," I mumbled through partially chewed celery. "Uh, what are you doing here?" I asked after swallowing the stringy vegetable.

"Your motorhome is out front. I live down the street."

"Oh." I couldn't believe she stood in front of me. I cursed myself for bringing it. But I'd been so excited to get baptized I couldn't wait for Lee to drive me.

Everyone cleaned up faster than I had ever seen Mormons move. The chairs were up, the kitchen wiped down, and the hallway lights were off in a matter of minutes. After the bishop pushed us out the door, he locked it and ran to his car. Only the RV and Keira's Mini Coop waited in the parking lot.

"Walk you to your car?" I asked.

"Sure."

We were silent as we walked the short distance. Twice I took a deep breath like I was going to say something. Both times I just sighed, losing my nerve. When I saw she was safe at her vehicle I turned to leave.

Keira cleared her throat, turning me around. She pointed at the car and said, "In!" With slumped shoulders I walked around the tiny car and fell into the seat.

We drove into Snowflake, finding a highway that looked like it led back out of town. I tugged on my collar. She turned into a housing complex climbing a plateau to the big white temple on a small hill. Lights surrounded the temple, making it look like a beacon in the dark. A golden man with a trumpet stood on the spire. They were always talking about the temple, but I'd had yet to come out and see it.

"Out," she said after parking.

"You're not going to leave me here, are you?"

"Out," she repeated.

I followed her toward the sound of running water. A fake waterfall over sandstones decorated that part of the parking lot in front of the main entrance to the building. We sat along the small retention mound of the pool. She watched the water streaming into the small pond.

"Who's the gold guy?" I asked, trying to break the awkward silence.

"You tell me; you're a Mormon now." She let out small laugh. "Brother Carroll."

"As of thirty minutes ago," I protested.

"Why?"

"Which why?" I asked.

"Why are you a Mormon now?" she demanded.

I didn't hold back, telling her everything. I told her about studying in California, about Aiko singing. Tears rolled down both our cheeks when I finished.

"You read a lot out there, huh?" she asked with a smile while wiping at her eyes.

I assumed a smile was a good thing. "Yeah," I exhaled, finally relaxing.

"That's Moroni." She motioned over her shoulder with her thumb.

"Oh, the guy at the end? Cool."

She shivered in the fall air. Seeing her in sweats and flip-flops, I scooted over to her and put my arm around her. My heart flipped when she let me.

"Did you think I was mad at you that day?" She turned toward me.

My mouth fell open. "You mean when you stomped off, leaving me at your sister's house wondering what I'd done wrong?"

"Well, when you put it like that."

"Yes," I said. "I did think that you were mad at me."

"Um, I'm sorry. I wasn't mad at you."

"Wait, you seemed pretty upset. My history with women leads me to believe that when they're mad, it's usually my fault."

"I wasn't mad at you." She looked up at me. "When you told me why you wanted to be baptized, I became furious with myself. All the things I'd said to you at church shot through my mind. It hurt because everything I said, strung you along to that decision."

"Meh, I guess a little." I tried to make her feel better.

"No, a lot. When I left you that afternoon, I beat myself up for how I was leading you to make a decision that I really shouldn't have been a part of. I also think that maybe I was desperate to love someone."

I pulled my arm away. "Ouch," I finally said.

"That's not exactly what I meant. Sorry. It's just that my relationship with Ryan left me . . . broken. I just want so badly to be loved that I feel like I took it from you too quickly."

"So why did you come to California?"

She sat still, looking up at the sky. "I wanted to tell you all of this that night."

"I finished the worst three weeks of my life and that's what you were going to tell me?"

"That's why I didn't. Lizzie wanted me to go out and surprise you so bad. She wouldn't relent, so I went . . . to make her leave me alone."

"Oh." I tilted my head, thinking of what she'd just said. "Ouch."

We both sat in silence for a moment. The cold air started to bite through my sweater.

"You know," I said, breaking the silence. "Tonight wasn't about you."

She looked up at me. "I'm sorry."

"Don't be, I guess. You're being honest."

"I just can't right now. Can we be friends?"

I tilted my head to look at her. Why would she ask that? "N-no." Of course we couldn't, not now. Who stays friends after love?

Her head dropped.

"I mean," I continued. "Let's go rock this tomorrow and go from there. We're still a team. I guess we could both use a win tomorrow."

"I could use a win," she said.

"Team?" I put my hand out.

"Team." She nodded, putting her hand on mine. "Okay," she said, standing up. "Tomorrow is a big day. We need to get ready."

Chapter 23

We made up a big crowd, bunched together at the starting line. Even with the sun in the sky, we felt the chill of the November morning. Random puffs of steam from the other competitors shot in the air. Those of us in the weight loss competition wore red headbands to set us apart. Keira and I had dressed as a team for the race. We both wore tight running pants she'd ordered, which went down to our mid-calves. I had scoffed at wearing something that looked like yoga pants, but after Keira had rambled on about cutting-edge mud obstacle material, I had let it go. Lizzie had tie-dyed two sleeveless running shirts for us, making us both cringe at wearing them. But we had nothing else that matched, and we figured they were just going to turn brown in the mud anyway. After looking at myself in a mirror, wearing spanks and tie-dye, I'd insisted on looking more ferocious. So she'd found blue skin paint and we'd Bravehearted our faces. On her forehead she also wrote "Taylor Trash" as a dig to Reggie. Her hair was tied back with the cornrows along the side of her head, making her appear even more intimidating.

The race wasn't just for those of us in the weight loss competition. Those of us losing weight had to do it, but the race was open to anyone. The competition organizers didn't want us cutting weight like fighters. To limit that, anyone who didn't finish the race would be disqualified. Trying to run for almost six and a half miles after cutting water weight was going to limit people like that. People like me. I would have done it if I were able.

Because of the race, I remained hydrated. That said, I didn't plan on drinking more water than I needed as I raced. The slightest ounce could determine the game. Blake—or Marty, as he was supposed to be called, looked good. His skin wrapped around his muscles. Jeremy, though still with loose skin, looked skinny as well. My belly sagged, but at least my ribs popped a little.

We met our opponents as we walked up to the finish line.

"Phil." Blake smiled.

"Bl . . . Marty," I replied.

"Keira." Reggie nodded with a big white smile.

"Reggie," she growled back.

Ryan just glared at me. He wore all black, including yoga pants like us. His muscles popped out of his tight black dri-wicking sleeveless shirt. A black sweatband crowned his head. He'd started growing back his Colonel Sanders goatee. Watching me, steam exploded out of his flaring nostrils. A vein thumped in his forehead.

Reggie and Kenny wore matching red dri-tech shirts. Reggie had arranged logos from sponsors all over their shirts, with nothing more prominent than First Street Fat Loss System. Reggie had a smirk on his face. Kenny's eyes darted around at all the racers as he fidgeted with his hands. When Reggie looked away, he mouthed "sorry" to me. I tilted my head, trying to figure out what he meant. Then Ryan stood between us, still glaring at me.

I'm not usually a vindictive guy, but I had to do something. "Team?" I asked Keira, putting my hand out. She replied with an excited grunt, dropping her hand on mine. Veins suddenly popped out of Ryan's neck. He pointed at me and then dragged his thumb across his neck. I rolled my eyes in response, mostly because he'd confirmed that he hadn't heard about our breakup.

"Racers!" Gina from the fitness association said into a bullhorn. "All weight losers will report to the big tent at the finish line. Are we ready?"

Everyone cheered in response—everyone but those of us involved in Keira and Reggie's rivalry. I took one last look at Ryan, whose nostrils flared at me again. He paced back and forth, clenching and unclenching his hands. Anyone with a brain would have been intimidated. I might have been a little cocky that morning. Everything was pretty uncertain, but I felt good. After all, what could he do? It was just a race.

Gina raised a starting pistol and her other arm in the air.

"Ready! Set!" She dropped her other arm. "Go!" she shouted as she pulled the trigger.

Keira bolted forward and I followed. We ran a half mile to the first obstacle. We dove into a mud bog covered with lines of barbed wire over it. Other racers had gotten there before us. That wasn't what mattered. It mattered that we got there before Reggie and Blake. Ryan followed us in, right on our heels.

We crawled through a few inches of mud with the barbed wire about two feet off the ground. My arms and legs clawed and plowed through the mud. One of my feet suddenly wouldn't go forward. I looked back to find Ryan's hand latched around my ankle. Keira shot forward without me. She got out and began running. Ryan pressed my foot deep into the mud. His hand moved up my legs and then over my back, crawling over me. Before he got past me, he pushed my face deep in the mud.

My hands were covered with mud and I couldn't wipe my blinded eyes. They wouldn't even open. I couldn't defend myself when his foot found my face as he slithered past me. Even though my eyes were closed, I could see a blinding white light when his heel made contact with my face. I gagged when I felt the bone of my nose crunch and grind. There was no choice but to keep moving forward. Even with the blinding pain, I couldn't do anything about it in the mud under barbed wire. I crawled out and took a knee at the end of the obstacle because I couldn't see. A volunteer ran up, putting a towel in my hand. I wiped my face with too much force and almost fell forward with the pain that shot through my nose. I cleared my eyes right as Reggie and Blake crawled out from under the barbed wire. Reggie laughed. Blake put his hands up, signaling to me that he didn't have any part in this.

Tears gathered in my eyelids from the violent pain of the hit. I brought my hand away from my nose to see blood gushing into the towel. I had never "seen red" before, as some people have described it. My blood pooling in the towel pushed me past red. My imagination conjured up all the stunts Ryan might try on Keira. I jumped up and sprinted toward him.

Jeremy had just crawled from under the wire. He had his GoPro around his head. His friends ran alongside the course, cheering for him. He panted pretty hard. I yelled at him to keep up. I figured he wasn't going to when I sprinted ahead of him.

I'd just about caught up to Ryan and Keira when they reached a cargo net. We had to climb to the top and then slide down black culverts. I watched Keira reach the top. She disappeared down the slide. Ryan almost got into the slide but then fell backwards. I think he was waiting for me to be just beneath him. His mass fell directly into my face. I just about screamed as his spine ground into my already-hurt nose. Reggie and Blake passed us again. They climbed up and disappeared into the culverts. Ryan turned right around and climbed again. Jeremy made it to the cargo net just as I started climbing for the second time.

I slid down the wet culvert and ran to catch up with them again. After another half mile, I found everyone bottlenecked at a ten-foot wall. Ryan crouched on his hands and knees while Reggie and Blake used him as a step and launched over. Keira ran, jumping at the wall. Her hands were too slippery and she kept losing her grip. She turned with a red face to yell at me when I ran up. She stopped herself; maybe the bloody nose silenced her. I cupped my hands by my knees, she stepped in, and I launched her up. Keira straddled the wall. Her hand dropped down to pull me up.

But then I heard the cheers of Jeremy's fans and froze. I knew Keira needed every second, but I remembered watching the poor kid the previous night, jumping, clawing, and hanging on the wall with no success. He thumped toward us, his loose skin flapping and waving beneath his shirt, his eyes opened wide in desperation, staring at the obstacle. When I saw him, I knew. Jeremy wasn't going to make it over the wall. I looked up into Keira's big, beautiful eyes. I ached to watch her cross that finish line before Reggie. She had worked so hard, and we were so close. Failure meant she had nothing here. The memory of reading something about bearing the burdens of others flashed through my mind.

My shoulders dropped and I growled. I couldn't do it. I pointed at Jeremy. "Just go!" I called to Keira.

He leaned over, dry heaving with a bright red face. I waved him forward, getting on my hands and knees. His foot landed on the small of my back. He struggled. I pushed to my feet to give him momentum to get over the wall. When I felt his feet leave my back, I looked up and saw Keira pulling him over. She reached down, offering me her hand again. I stepped back. With a yell, I bolted at the wall, throwing my hand up. My legs pumped up the wood while my free hand clawed for the top of the wall, where she caught me and pulled. We landed on the other side without Reggie, Blake, or Ryan in view.

We looked at each other. "Let's find Ryan!" I roared over the cheers of Jeremy's entourage. I reached out, grabbing her hand. I pulled her forward. The rage I felt kept me in pace with her. We leapt over giant hay bales. We washed away some of the brown wading through water filled with thousands of ice cubes. We swung on a thick rope across a waist-deep mud pit.

We finally caught up with Reggie, Blake, and Ryan when we started the last mile. With only one obstacle left, Keira blazed forward, mud splattering out of her wet hair and caking her face and her clothes, the happiest I had ever seen her.

On the other hand, I had drained myself of energy. My lungs burned. The muscles in my legs screamed at me to stop. All the hatred pumping through me that had gotten me to this point had fizzled. I repeated to myself to put one foot in front of the other. I only found comfort in the fact that my nose had at least stopped bleeding. My head felt like it floated, probably from the loss of blood.

Ryan looked back and saw us. He slowed down to hit the final obstacle the same time as us. A line of old, beat-up cars blocked the course. Not just a couple of cars blocking the race. About forty yards of old rusty cars we had to pass. The organizers had arranged them in the cruelest way possible. Some had their front wheels leaning on the trunk of another. One car sat on its side. They'd somehow flipped another upside down. My thundering heart fell into my stomach seeing that last obstacle.

Keira ran straight at them. She jumped and bounded over hoods and tires. Ryan matched my speed as I approached. Each time I tried to jump on a hood or a roof, he would fall back to step on my heel.

On the last car, I'd had enough. I sprinted to the hood of a rusty Buick. He had to speed up to try and kick my heel. Instead of jumping onto the car, I leaned over. His foot missed me, but his momentum carried him forward and he folded over my back. With a yell I stood up straight, flipping him onto the hood. He slid across the hood, tearing his shirt, and landed on his butt on the other side of the car.

"Get a tetanus booster!" I shouted, jumping over him. It wasn't my best material. Almost finished with the last half mile of the race, I was too tired for a quality one-liner.

Without Ryan blocking her, Keira sprinted forward to catch Reggie. Everyone cheered by the finish line. Lee and Lizzie had driven the Bago to the race. They'd parked it along the finish line with chairs on the top, where I saw them jumping and screaming.

I caught up to Kenny Blake about fifty yards from the finish, but our race had finished. It was over. Now it was up to the numbers. He nodded as we matched each other's slowing pace. We didn't say anything for a moment. Our feet thudded through the grass. Both our heads dripped sweat.

"I didn't know that the meathead was going to do all that!" he shouted as we neared the finish line. "He was only supposed to slow you two down."

I waved him off as we ran on. Someone had won, making people go crazy. There was too much mayhem to see if Keira had slipped through. Blake and I continued to jog in silence. When I got to the finish line, a volunteer ushered me into a large white tent. Another volunteer wrapped a tape measure around me. Her hand covered the numbers. She pointed me ahead to another volunteer, who watched me get on the scale. The red numbers flashed 183.4.

I stuck my finger in the air to do the math. Fifty-seven point six pounds. You wouldn't see that amount on a big TV competition. It wouldn't be the winning number on one, either. With my weight at the start of the competition, that made my total percentage . . . I stuck my hand back in the air. I estimated it at about twenty-four percent. I had lost almost a quarter of my body weight. Things could be good. They never did say how they used the belly measurement, so I still couldn't tell what the final number would be.

When the adrenaline of the race had worn off I felt my nose throbbing. An emergency medical technician sat off to one side of the tent, tapping on his phone. I guess the association thought some of us were going to die. I walked right up to him and pointed to my nose.

"Oh!" he shouted, jumping from his seat. "What? How?"

"Will you doing something about it, please?"

He winced and then got to work. I held back tears and shrieks of pain as he poked and prodded it. After looking at my nose, he gagged at the swelling ball on my face. My teeth ground as he shoved cotton up my nose. I marveled at the size of the huge ibuprofen tablets he gave me. Would these ruin my kidneys now, or in the morning? Finally, his only other treatment was to hand me an ice pack. "It's definitely broken." I stomped toward the exit after hearing his astute medical opinion. Of course it was broken. "You need to see a doctor!" he shouted as I left the tent.

The more I walked, the shakier my legs became. I nearly collapsed when Keira ran up and jumped in my arms. Her shoulder brushed against my nose, making me scream in pain.

"I'm so sorry!" she shouted, jumping away from me. Keira tilted her head to look at my nose. I quickly covered my face again with the ice.

"So?" I asked. The ice pack muted my question.

"I won!" she shouted, raising her arms in triumph. I tried to shout back, but it turned to a moan. "So what happened?"

I pointed at Ryan, who marched past, limping and glaring at me. A rip in his muddy shirt he wore exposed his six-pack. I smiled when Keira didn't seem to notice.

Jeremy walked up behind us. "You guys have to see this!" He replayed some video on the tiny screen of his GoPro. Keira gasped watching Ryan flip over the old car where a jagged edge tore his shirt open. She laughed watching him land on his butt. When I had bolted past him he started screaming, "I broke my butt!"

Jeremy giggled and pointed at Ryan, who turned and limped off. But with each step he took he grunted in pain.

When we were finished, Lee and Lizzie walked up cheering.

"Oh!" they both shouted in unison. The reaction to my face was beginning to be slightly embarrassing. Aiko began to cry.

***

We gathered around a big flatbed trailer. A cool breeze drifted through the crowd. I wore a towel around my shoulders to stay warm. Two small black speakers flanked Gina. She held a microphone attached by a cord to the speakers. I stared at the big cardboard check for eight thousand dollars leaning against her leg.

"Ladies and gentlemen. The time you've waited almost three months for has finally arrived. We are proud to present this check of eight thousand dollars to the winner of the first Taylor-Snowflake Fitness Association Weight Loss Competition." She stuck her tongue out. "That's a mouthful."

Keira, I assumed as a teammate, squeezed my hand. My heart began pounding again, both out of anxiety and because Keira had touched me.

"Now, this has been tallied based on percentage lost, not on total pounds lost. We are going to call up the top three losers!"

Everyone laughed at her pun.

"Phil Carroll, Jeremy Higgins, and Marty Jenkins. Please come up onto the stage."

The three of us climbed up. We were tired and sore, and everything ached as I climbed up onto the trailer. My heart continued to pound as I waited to hear my fate.

Jeremy hoisted himself up onto the flatbed. He lay back to swing his legs up but just stayed where he was. When he didn't get up, I decided just to collapse and sit. Blake sat behind me and leaned up against me.

Everyone laughed at us.

"Funny boys," Gina proceeded. "Now, none of you will leave empty-handed. The second runner-up will be given this one-hundred-dollar gift card to Basha's. Don't take that straight to the bakery!"

Everyone laughed again. Was this town deprived of humor? Maybe I just couldn't see anything to laugh at while my body ached and my nose throbbed.

"The first runner-up will receive this five-hundred-dollar gas card from Giant!"

Everyone clapped.

"Now, let's get on with it. The winner with the biggest fat loss percentage is…"

This was it. I had traveled from the Midwest. I had met the woman of my dreams, then lost her. I'd gone through three weeks of pure hell getting back into jiu-jitsu. I'd become a Mormon. All for this one moment. My life had completely changed forever because of this one last competition.

"Jeremy Higgins, with twenty-six percent fat loss!"

Kenny's head fell backward on my shoulder. He started to curse. I snorted and then winced in pain. Then I giggled, but that turned to chuckling. Finally I fell back, clutching my nose in excruciating pain and hysterical laughter. Kenny looked down at me, laughing as well.

"What's so funny?" he choked out.

"He wouldn't have made it over the wall!" I burst through my laughter. "I helped him over the wall!" Regardless of the stabbing pain in my nose, I lost control, rolling back and forth on the dusty wood planks of the flatbed.

Nobody heard us since they had all begun cheering. Their hometown hero vlogger jumped up while we laughed. Miraculously finding a second wind, he danced around the flatbed. Three girls rushed onto the makeshift stage. They hugged him, kissed him, and started fighting over him. In the scuffle they pushed Gina away from the microphone. No one cared about her anymore. Jeremy began speaking into the mic, thanking a whole list of people. Gina, recognizing that she couldn't take the mic back, walked over to us with the gift cards.

"Phil, you're second with twenty-four percent, and Marty had twenty-three and a half," she said, handing us our gift cards.

When he realized what that meant, he joined me in hysterics. "So you would have won?"

"Yes," I whimpered as my laughter subsided.

I felt Blake's hand come over my head. "We don't have a Basha's in Kansas. You take it," he muttered.

"You want to eat with us tonight?" I muttered back.

"Yeah. Why not," he said, rolling to his stomach then getting on all fours. "My stuff is packed and ready go. I don't think Reggie will be fun to be around right now." He crawled off the trailer.

Kenny and Lee helped me climb off the flatbed. I handed the Basha's card to Lizzie, who didn't mind at all that I'd invited Blake to come eat with us. We piled into the RV, with Blake's car following us home . . . after a stop at Basha's for more food.

Chapter 24

Lee got his grill ready for burgers when we got to his house. While Lizzie prepped the rest of the food, Keira showered and changed in the house and Kenny and I did the same in the Winnebago.

About twenty minutes after Lee started getting his grill ready for burgers, Jeremy arrived alone. He hobbled across Lee's yard with the same type of sore legs Blake and I were enduring. We stood on the porch, leaning against the railing and watching the wind sweep through the dry grass. Each of us had a long stem of grass in our mouths.

"Did you know you two are going out of style?" Jeremy asked.

"What?" Blake turned to him with his mouth open, the grass sticking between his cheek and teeth.

"Yeah man, it's not about the competitions anymore. This competition will keep on giving. My vlog, Twitter account, Snapchat, and Facebook accounts all earned about three grand in ad revenue. Good Morning America is going to fly me to New York to appear on their show. And they're going to pay me. I'm in negotiations for an e-book deal. I'm estimating a ten-grand advance." Jeremy slapped us both on the shoulders and walked inside.

Blake and I looked at each other, our mouths wide open, then out at the giant white clouds sailing over us.

"I know I'm done," I confessed. "Mormon now, gotta be honest."

"So it's true? I heard you got dunked. Maybe he's right. Maybe I am a dying breed." He spit out the grass, then looked out at the shadows the sun cast as it sank. "No, there'll always be fat people willing to lose weight for money." He slapped his hand down on my shoulder then turned to follow Jeremy back inside.

Uncle Tim pulled up in a small tan pickup a few minutes later.

"Howdy, *oji*," I called as he walked up the porch.

"Hey, *oi*. How'd it go?"

"Eh, well, not so good. I didn't win."

"So no Japan?"

"Not yet."

"Are you still running?"

"Nowhere to run to now. Let's go eat," I said, leading him through the door.

When Lee finally finished the burgers, Jeremy, Blake, and I rushed over to the counter. We practically pushed Lee and Keira out of the way to get there. Potato salad, macaroni and cheese, sweet potato pie, and cornbread lined Lizzie's island counter. She'd turned her kitchen into a foodie Pinterest paradise. The smell alone forced my eyes to roll back in my head.

After Keira said a prayer, we dieters turned the counter into a trough. Lizzie forced a smile. I could tell in her eyes she wanted to send us outside where pigs belong. She settled into a chair at the table with her back to us while we gorged. I was too ravenous to give in to any expectation to be polite and courteous. Shreds of food flew all over the counter. Some sort of sauce dripped down my chin. I used a chip to scrape it off—I didn't waste it by wiping it with a napkin when I could be stuffing in my mouth. We treated the edges of our plates as mere guidelines. If food fell onto the table, we just stabbed it with a fork and pressed on.

After an hour of satisfying our appetites, we were civil enough to do the cleaning before everyone sat down in the living room. Jeremy and Blake lay on the floor clutching their stomachs. I sat against the couch, with no energy to defend myself as Aiko decorated my hair with bows and clips. Keira sat next to her, handing her the pinkest bows she could find. Lizzie nuzzled into Lee as they rocked in the recliner. We all stewed over a YouTube playlist of Billy Joel music.

A knock at the door interrupted "Piano Man." Lee got up, pausing the music. He opened the door and we all watched Gina come in.

"Wow, you're all here?" she asked.

"I invited them over to have salads," Lee said.

"Hi," we said in agonized unison.

"Well, that's funny," Gina said. "Well, *Coach* Akiyama. I've brought your check."

"Thanks, Gina," he said.

"Congratulations on coaching the winning loser." She laughed at her word choice. "We'll have a featured spot of your gym up on our website tomorrow. And congratulations to all of you and your new lives." She waved, leaving us gawking at Lee.

When he closed the door, Lee jumped back a little when he saw the looks on our faces. "What?" he cried.

"Explain yourself!" Lizzie snapped.

"Well, everyone was hustling everyone else. So I talked to Jeremy and we teamed up," Lee declared, with Jeremy nodding in agreement.

"But, I needed that." Keira mumbled, expressionless.

"I know, sis. I'm sorry. You were all worried about your own things. And Phil even said that it would be great for people to see the winner come out of my gym when he first got here. Not to mention, I've been worried about Lizzie for a while. And how else was I supposed to book a vacation to Puerto Rico?" Lee smiled.

Lizzie squealed. She ran to Lee, jumping into his arms.

"Babe, I love you," Lee said. "The way you take care of me and Aiko is something I can never repay. Even when I kept trying to convince you that we needed to make Phil find a new place to park his rig, you kept insisting we needed to look out for him."

"Hey!" I protested.

Lee continued without listening to me. "You took in your sister after he-who-will-not-be-named, then got her back on her feet. You went out of your way to set her up and arrange a proposal. Although…"

"HEY!" Keira and I shouted.

"That's the kind of person you are. It's always about helping other people. This is the last amount I needed to take you on a real vacation. Everything is going to be paid for. No cooking, no cleaning, no yelling, no washing clothes for two whole weeks."

"Oh babe, I love you too. You're the best hustler in the world," she said, giving him a light peck on the cheek. Then her lips plowed into his.

Lee broke free and yelled, "Everyone get out of my house!" We just looked at him, still in shock. "Come on guys, please leave!" he whined.

We all helped each other up. Blake and I almost had to roll Jeremy out the door. He'd binged harder than we had. We'd be able to go back to eating normally again. Jeremy had to maintain the loss to keep up his long con. So he'd kept eating long after common sense told him to stop. Lee slammed the door on us when we were all out. We heard him run through the house.

"Blake, my couch is available if you need a place to stay," I told him. "It's open."

"I'll take you up on that, thanks," he said. I watched him disappear into the Bago.

Jeremy left. Keira and I waved as his headlights disappeared down the gravel road. We sat on the steps for a while. She frowned, staring at the dark hills with slumped shoulders.

"You know what we did to ourselves, right?" she asked.

"You mean with Jeremy and the wall? Yep. You know, that was the costliest decision I have ever made. That was a ten-thousand-dollar choice for us." Keira whistled at the total. "But, even with Lee and Jeremy reverse hustling us . . . he looked like an honest kid trying to take care of himself. And in the end, that's what he did. I guess I don't feel that bad about it."

"Not even a little?" she elbowed my side.

My finger went into the air. "Well, I guess maybe a little." We both laughed until I groaned in pain, but that made Keira laugh harder.

"So what will you do now?" she asked.

"I think I'll go home. Spend time with Mom through New Year's. Finish saving up for my trip to Japan with a real job. What about you?"

"Lee took my money."

"I think you'll be all right. You did coach the first runner-up. You won the race. So you have some reputation, and you won Taylor as your clientele."

"I needed the money as start-up."

"Yeah." I laughed, thinking again about helping Jeremy over the wall. "You sure did." There were millions of stars in the sky twinkling in those eyes. With nothing else to say, she turned and walked to her car. I watched as her taillights became tiny red dots in the night.

"So, what are you going to do about her?" Tim's voice made me jump. I turned to find him relaxing in one of the rocking chairs.

"What can I do about her? She made her choice, and it wasn't me. I've accepted it. I'm going home to set things straight."

"You sure you're not running again?"

"How is that running?"

"Where will Keira be?"

"It doesn't matter now."

"Well, okay." He stood up and walked over to me. "Good luck." He slapped my shoulder and walked out into the night.

***

The Winnebago's engine hummed under my feet. A vast expanse of high desert grassland surrounded the black stretch of asphalt I rode. Green cedar bushes dotted the landscape as I followed the giant blue sky ahead of me.

I didn't know what Keira was doing that morning, miles behind me. Although whatever it was she was doing, I wished I was there. I wished that her plans for recovering from the loss had somehow involved me. I groaned—not from my broken nose or sore muscles, but from longing for her to press her lips on mine just one more time. *Oji* was right: she was back there and I was driving away from her.

But without her, I drove forward to figure out what the word *home* meant. A weight of uncertainty that I hadn't felt in years rode on my shoulders. It had kept me up most of the night.

The bishop and the missionaries had already called the ward at home. So a new network waited for me. But what did I have to offer? I'd been fooling people for so long that I had years' worth of nothing an employer would ever want. A thirty-something guy who loved jiu-jitsu and counting money was a combination that seemed anything but lucrative to a potential boss. Before driving off, I had re-taped my postcard of Japan to the dashboard.

So I drove on under the blue dome, still trying to figure out how to get there.

Special Thanks

Thank you to:

Mandi, my best friend, lover, mother of my daughters, Netflix buddy, and eternal companion.

Tara Holladay for letting me bug you with tons of questions and for finding a great editor for me. tmholladay.com

Jana Miller I thought I had a decent story. Thank you for the advice, coaching, and sorry you had your work cut out for you when you edited all the bad grammar. the-writers-assistant.com

Mom and Dad for all the support. Thanks mom for puking for nine months while you constructed me. Thanks dad for all the times you spanked me and told me not to be stupid.

My (M)ANWA group for the encouragement and invaluable critiques. anwa-lds.org

Finally, thank you Bank of America female coworkers that I destroyed in our own weight-loss competition. Had I not lost twenty pounds and won the ninety-dollar purse; I would never have come up with this idea.

About the Author

Tyson Abaroa was born in Provo, UT but raised in Gilbert, AZ. His freshman year of high school his English teacher Mrs. Pershing assigned him to write an essay about what he would be when he grew up. He listed a step-by-step plan on how he would become World Dictator. This should have been his first clue that his imagination needed to be cultivated. However, in July 2001 between his junior and senior year of high school he enlisted in the Marine Corps Reserves. After graduating high school, boot camp, and MOS school, his unit was deployed to build a fuel hose line in support of the invasion of Iraq. After this deployment he served in the Chile Santiago East Mission. He married soon after returning home. Just before his first anniversary he was deployed again; his time to Djibouti, Africa as part of a provisional security company. Tyson's ADHD has led to an eclectic career after the Marine Corps. He has been a credit card collector, a claims processor, and now a Track Director for USA BMX. He draws from his diverse experiences and develops stories to write about in his spare time. He lives in Gilbert, AZ with his wife and two daughters.

Reference

The Book of Mormon. Ed. Church of Jesus Christ of Latter-day Saints. Salt Lake City: Church of Jesus Christ of Latter-day Saints, 2006. Print.

CPSIA information can be obtained
at www.ICGtesting.com
Printed in the USA
LVHW03s2300200918
590878LV00010B/326/P

9 781978 173248